"Why are you staring at me?" Garrick asked.

When Elise didn't answer, he rubbed his chin. "I suppose I need a shave."

"You hate that, don't you, those seven or eight hours when you're not in complete control, and your beard grows without your permission." Her voice was low and husky as she taunted him. "I always liked you best in the morning, before you slipped into pin-striped perfection. You're not quite so civilized then."

She experienced a moment of triumph when his eyes flared. Then with a sudden movement he shifted, reversing their bodies so he held her pinned beneath him. Grasping her chin, he rubbed his thumb across her bottom lip with rough strokes. "Are you sure you know what you're doing?" he asked.

She wanted to say *no*, she had no idea what she was doing. She only knew she was unexpectedly afraid.

As if he recognized her uncertainty, his fingers tightened on her chin. "Too late, Elise," he said with a harsh laugh. His mouth closed over hers before he had finished speaking. Taken off guard, she struggled for a moment, but when he nipped at her lower lip, a surge of white-hot desire shot through her, taking control of her body away from her, parting her lips. She had expected anger, and she could have handled that. But this was hunger, blatant and so powerful she had no defenses against it. . . .

WHAT ARE *LOVESWEPT* ROMANCES?

They are stories of true romance and touching emotion. We believe those two very important ingredients are constants in our highly sensual and very believable stories in the *LOVESWEPT* line. Our goal is to give you, the reader, stories of consistently high quality that may sometimes make you laugh, sometimes make you cry, but are always fresh and creative and contain many delightful surprises within their pages.

Most romance fans read an enormous number of books. Those they truly love, they keep. Others may be traded with friends and soon forgotten. We hope that each *LOVESWEPT* romance will be a treasure—a "keeper." We will always try to publish

LOVE STORIES YOU'LL NEVER FORGET
BY AUTHORS YOU'LL ALWAYS REMEMBER

The Editors

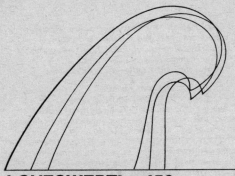

LOVESWEPT® · 456

Billie Green
Starbright

BANTAM BOOKS
NEW YORK · TORONTO · LONDON · SYDNEY · AUCKLAND

STARBRIGHT

A Bantam Book / March 1991

If you would be interested in receiving protective vinyl
covers for your Loveswept books, please write to this address
for information:

Loveswept
Bantam Books
P.O.Box 985
Hicksville, NY 11802

ISBN 0-553-44101-9

Published simultaneously in the United States and Canada

PRINTED IN THE UNITED STATES OF AMERICA

OPM 0 9 8 7 6 5 4 3 2 1

To Linda Burch and Nancy Craig.
I promise I'm writing as fast as I can.
Thanks for waiting.

One

"Mother—" Elise said firmly. "Mother, *let me talk*!"

On the other end of the telephone line Mona breathed a weak "Really!" before lapsing into offended silence.

Swallowing a laugh, Elise promised herself she'd keep her voice suitably contrite for the rest of this conversation. "You won't even miss me," she said. "You have hundreds of friends, a very distinguished husband, and three other children who adore you. The whole world is ready, willing, and able to help you celebrate your birthday. You don't need me there." She paused to give reason a chance to penetrate her mother's emotional fog. "It just comes at a bad time this year. I'm in the middle of half a dozen crises here at work and—"

"Not to mention a marriage you're doing your level best to destroy," Mona interjected.

Déjà vu, Elise thought. She should have known her mother would get to this subject. "Didn't we cover this topic last night when you called to nag me? Give it up, Ma. You're beating a dead horse."

"How many times have I asked you not to call me 'Ma'? You only do it to remind me of your uncivilized upbringing. And a 'dead horse' is a fine way to talk about the—"

"If I hear the words 'sacred bonds of matrimony' come out of your mouth one more time, I swear I'm going to scream. I mean it, Mother," Elise warned, breaking all her vows to be sweet-voiced and contrite in this conversation. "It's *my* marriage. Mine and Garrick's. It's over when we say it's over. It has nothing to do with you."

For the next few seconds Mona made little huffing noises, then, with a familiar whine in her voice, she said, "I don't understand you, Elise. You're not throwing over some ignorant laborer with dirty fingernails. This is Garrick Hewitt Fane, the most brilliant criminal lawyer in the country. You simply do not dump men like Garrick."

Since Mona gave all the indications of settling in for a good, long hectoring session, Elise swiveled her chair around to face her desk and picked up the contract she had been checking before her mother's call had interrupted her.

"We're legally separated," Elise said as she

scanned the document. "That doesn't exactly constitute dumping."

"You can't tell me Garrick wants this. It was all your idea." Her mother exhaled an exasperated breath. "You had everything, Elise. Social position, wealth, not to mention Garrick himself."

"But you *are* going to mention him, aren't you?" Elise said with a tiny twitch of a smile.

"Someone needs to. No man could have a more impeccable background. He's one of the New Hampshire Fanes, Elise! A man like that could have anyone he wanted. And although I will never understand why he chose you, he did. The man's a saint. A genuine saint. Don't try to tell me you're easy to live with, because I know better. Garrick couldn't possibly have approved of the way you kept your maiden name when you started your little model agency. But did he stop you? Did he raise even one objection?"

Elise knew it would be less than useless to point out to her mother that they had discussed this subject on the average of once a month for the past two years. When the spirit moved Mona, she thought nothing of chastising Elise for something she had done as an infant.

"Garrick knows why I kept my maiden name, Mother," she said patiently. "Come to think of it, so do you. Even though you would never lower yourself so far as to become personally involved in business, I'm pretty sure you understand the precepts. I was a model," she said slowly, as though explaining to a child. "My name, Elise Adler Bright, became known in the industry. It would have been foolish for me not to take advantage of the modest amount of fame I earned. Now, can we let the subject drop for a week or so, at which time I'll explain it to you all over again?"

"I don't believe I like your tone."

Elise laughed softly. "And I don't believe I like the way you constantly interfere in my life. Want to call it even?"

"Interfere? *Interfere?* Is that what you call it? When from nothing less than unselfish concern, I'm trying to keep you from making the biggest mistake of your life?"

"Since my little agency is doing fine, I take it we're back on my marriage," Elise said. "Look, Ma— Sorry. Look, Mother, if I had a couple of spare lives, I'd live one of them only for you, honestly I would. But I don't. I have just one life. And I'm not going to waste any more of it on trying to make you comfortable."

"No one's asking you to waste your life. If you're finding your marriage a little dull right now, I can understand that, darling. But there are ways, Elise. There are ways to add excitement to your life without ruining your marriage in the process."

Reading the contract and listening to Mona at the same time must have slowed Elise's mental processes, because it took a moment for the suggestion to sink in. When it did, Elise laughed. She rocked back in her leather chair and laughed, long and hard, while her mother sputtered indignantly.

"This is the fabled motherly advice people are always talking about?" Elise asked finally as she wiped helpless tears from her eyes. "This is the maternal wisdom I've been waiting so long to hear from you? 'Go out and get a little on the side'—that's it, Mother?"

"One day . . . one day, Elise, your peculiar sense of humor is going to rebound on you," Mona said stiffly. "Must you be so crude? I'm simply trying to help. I'm trying to give you the benefit of my experience. You have to approach marriage with a clear head and distinct goals. And you never let go of a marriage until it no longer has anything to offer. Where do you think I would be today if I had let myself be swayed by personal preferences and sentimental notions? I wouldn't have married even one of your fathers."

"I only had one father." Elise's voice was distracted because she had finally spotted the clause that was causing trouble for one of her models. "I never even met your first husband, but every time you talk about 'dear Randal' you call him my father. He was Jason and Sharon's father. And Albie fathered Trish. My father— Daniel, in case you've forgotten—came between those two. And while I don't doubt that either Albie or your present husband could have fathered me, Randal Thornton died three years before I was born. It's biologically impossible for him to have been my father."

A moment of silence crackled across the line before Mona said, "Are you questioning my morals?"

"No, darling," Elise said gently. "I'm afraid there are no questions involved. The answers came to me, like a mystical message appearing on the wall, the first time I caught you in bed with someone other than your husband of the moment. And I have to tell you, it seems a little strange to hear you objecting to my divorce when you've divorced so often yourself."

This time the silence was searing, Mona's way of letting Elise know that she had once again crossed the line of acceptable behavior.

"If you are so contemptuous of my lifestyle," said Mona, her voice rigid, "it's rather ironic that you chose the same kind of marriage."

"Not ironic," Elise said. "It's sick. Which is why I'm doing my damnedest to get out of it. Look, I didn't mean to hurt your feelings, Mother. My peculiar sense of humor, as you call it, just got the better of me."

Almost immediately Elise knew that her apology had been the wrong move. The first rule of survival was never to let a circling vulture see that you were weakening.

"If you truly want to make amends," said Mona, diving down for the kill, "come to my birthday party. You never miss my birthday, Elise. People will talk if you're not here. They'll think we've quarreled."

Shaking her head in defeat, Elise said, "We certainly can't have people talking, can we? All right, Mother, you win. It's going to take some first-class maneuvering, but I'll be there. Look,

I've got another call coming in, so I have to hang up now."

And you can go annoy someone else, Elise thought as she replaced the receiver.

Garrick leaned back in his chair, an indulgent smile twitching at his strong lips as he held the telephone loosely to his ear. "Yes, Mona," he said again. "Of course, Mona."

After another fifteen minutes of the one-sided conversation, Mona paused and said, "I must say, I wish my daughter would show as much consideration. Well, to be perfectly frank, I wish she liked me half as much as you do, Garrick. You will come to my birthday party, won't you? Really, it won't be the same without you. You know how much I enjoy showing off my famous son-in-law. And we don't have to tell anyone about Elise's foolishness." She paused. "I've never understood her, you know. Sometimes it's impossible for me to believe she's actually the fruit of my womb. She doesn't look anything like me, and she can be so *difficult*."

The self-pitying, slightly pompous tone, Garrick knew, meant that Mona was now going to tackle what had become her favorite subject. He listened in silence as she criticized and condemned Elise's behavior. Although his mother-in-law always had approved of him, he knew she could become vicious the moment she was crossed. And for some reason, Mona saw his and Elise's separation as a personal insult.

"Mona . . . *Mona!* Don't you ever stop for breath?" he teased. "I appreciate your concern. I really do. But Elise is a grown woman. She has to make these decisions on her own."

"How can you be so tolerant? So forgiving?"

Garrick rubbed his temple with two fingers, frowning at the persistent headache. "There's nothing to forgive. Elise simply needs time alone to think about her plans for the future or maybe rethink them."

"Is that what she told you?" Mona's tone was derisive. "It's not like her to beat around the bush. Heaven knows she's blunt enough with me. She told me, not an hour ago, that your marriage was over. And you won't believe what she told me last night. She said—"

When Mona broke off, Garrick shifted his position restlessly. He knew she wanted him to urge her to continue. She wanted a show of interest on his part. He wouldn't encourage her to repeat Elise's confidences, he told himself. His wife had a right to her privacy, and he would respect that right.

But in the next moment words came out of his mouth of their own volition. "What did she say?"

"Well," said Mona, managing to make the word portentous, "when I pointed out what she was giving up and asked what on earth she was looking for, she said, 'Love.' *Love*, Garrick. Have you ever heard anything so ridiculous? I don't know how I kept from laughing right in her face."

"You find that funny?" he murmured.

"Don't you? She has the most wonderful husband in the world, a husband who gives her anything she wants. She has a position in society that most women would kill for. How could she . . ."

Garrick kept the receiver pressed to his ear, but for the next ten minutes he didn't listen. He let Mona ramble on, drifting from one complaint to the next. Finally he broke in to tell her he had a luncheon appointment.

After hanging up, he swung his chair around so that he faced the large window behind his desk. For a long time he simply sat there, staring at the Dallas skyline, then he abruptly got to his feet and walked out of his office.

Elise scratched her nose with the end of her pen. Then, realizing she had used the wrong end, she rubbed the ink off as she went over her schedule for the third time, trying to fit in her mother's birthday party. Since Mona lived in Springfield, Missouri, she would have to free up at least three days.

It still irritated Elise to think of the way she had given in to her mother when she had sworn she wouldn't. What was worse, she had given in for all the wrong reasons. She had agreed to go to the annual birthday celebration simply to keep Mona off the subject of Garrick.

For the past three months Elise had been trying to keep her husband out of her thoughts as much as possible. Here, at her office, she usually managed it. When she was at home, all alone in that big house, it was more difficult. Only the night before, as she tried to watch an episode of a TV miniseries in which one of her models had a brief part, she had suddenly found herself reliving the day she had met Garrick. It was the day that had changed her life.

"No . . . no, Elise, turn just a little to the left . . . that's it, let your hair blow across your face. Judas priest, not the whole freaking mess, just a few strands. You're not supposed to look like a hurricane victim. That's it. That's *it*! You're wonderful. You're absolutely wonderful!"

As Luther, the photographer, screamed out his frustration, his anger, and his euphoria, and as the lights assaulted her, Elise turned toward the fan, her expression reflecting only the cool, understated sexuality that was necessary for the shoot. She didn't ask what kind of hotel had a strong breeze blowing in the lobby. She didn't ask why the same lobby contained a live cheetah and enough greenery to film a Tarzan movie. Those questions had to do with reality, and she had learned early in her career not only not to ask questions relating to reality, but not to ask questions of any kind. Models weren't supposed to have brains. Brains got in the way. A body that could make absurd clothes look chic and a face that could make outlandish makeup look "now" were all that were required.

"Swing to the side . . . that's good. That's

good. Raise your arm—No, *no*!" Luther screamed. "Bend your elbow and drape your arm over your head. For Pete's sake, Elise, throw back your head just a little and frame your face with your arm. That's it. Good . . . good . . . *fantastic*!"

While maintaining her dreamy expression, Elise directed her gaze beyond Luther, beyond the technicians and equipment, and found herself staring into navy-blue eyes that looked as if they could see all the way to forever.

She didn't hear the photographer's next commands. Everything was lost in a stranger's eyes, midnight eyes that seemed to be asking questions, some that confused her, some that thrilled her. She felt her breasts heave in reaction and heat spread through her. Although she didn't move, her body felt as though it was being pulled in the man's direction.

"Elise, *Elise*! Where are you? Are you paying attention? That's the wrong look. Totally wrong. It's too basic. Too earthy. This is a study in contrasts. Come on, dear heart, give me the sophistication . . . give me the freaking refinement. Oh, jeez, Louise. She's sweating! Hannah! Hannah, get over there and powder her down, then touch up her lip makeup."

The stranger with the night-blue eyes smiled at Luther's disgusted tones, and the smile was only part of the silent conversation he was having with Elise. Without words, they agreed Luther was an extraordinarily silly man, and they decided they would get away from the photographer and his crew as soon as possible.

Hours later, after the shoot, when Luther finally gave Elise permission to be human, Garrick was waiting for her. On the surface, their conversation was the kind that ordinarily took place between two people meeting for the first time—they exchanged names, discovered they were both from Dallas, and agreed that, although he often came to New York, their meeting was quite a coincidence. But the ordinary conversation was only a cover for something that was in no way ordinary. A vibrant, compelling energy was surging between them, binding them inexplicably.

During dinner that same night, she told him she was tired of modeling, of doing what other people told her to do. She wanted to start her own model agency, and she wanted to do it her way. She would treat her models as individuals, as human beings rather than commodities, even if it meant making less money than she might.

Garrick showed the correct amount of interest in her plans. He even told her a little about what she would be up against if she started her agency in Dallas, as she planned. Afterward he told her about himself, about his career as a criminal lawyer, about some of the unusual cases he had handled, and she asked all the questions a new acquaintance was expected to ask.

But beneath the polite talk, the silent conversation continued. Every time his navy-blue eyes met hers, he told her that he wanted her. He told her he wanted to hold her naked in his arms and spend the entire night giving her pleasure. He told her that touching her would be an unbearably beautiful experience.

And while they talked aloud about the differences between Dallas and New York, her green eyes told him she had never regretted so much that she wasn't the kind of woman who could let a stranger make love to her.

Garrick stayed in New York for a week, and they were together as much as their separate schedules allowed. They didn't kiss. Not once. They didn't even hold hands. They both knew, as surely as if the words had been spoken aloud, that a single touch would be one touch too many. And if they ever kissed, neither of them would be able to draw back.

The night before he was due to fly back to Dallas, Garrick took her to a musical review followed by supper at a quiet, chic little restaurant. Then they walked and talked for hours. It was after three when he finally returned Elise to her apartment. As they stood in front of her door, there was an unfamiliar anxiety in the air between them, a feeling of apprehension that was apparent every time their eyes met.

All evening Elise had managed to keep her tone light, but now, when she said good-bye, her lip trembled. For a long, tense moment, Garrick stared at her mouth, then he slowly reached out to touch the sensitive flesh with his fingertip.

As a barely audible groan escaped her, she

closed her eyes and swayed toward him. She couldn't help it.

And that was all it took. Seconds later they were inside her apartment, and he was carrying her toward her bedroom.

"This is— This is what you want?" His deep voice was hoarse, urgent, as he pressed heated lips against the smooth flesh of her neck. "I'll stop— I think I can still stop, if you're not sure."

"I was sure the first night," she whispered huskily, "but I didn't understand what was happening. I still don't understand."

He let her slide to her feet beside the bed, and catching her chin between the thumb and fingers of his right hand, he stared into her eyes. "Maybe we're not supposed to understand. Maybe we're not supposed to ask questions. The only thing that worries me— Elise, I have to know you won't regret this tomorrow. I can't take such a risk. If this is going to ruin things between us, I'll leave right now."

"You can't." The forceful, almost angry words were out of her mouth instantly. "You can't leave." Pushing her hands beneath his jacket, she twined her arms around his back and molded her body to his. "Can you?"

He sucked in a harsh breath, and his hips moved reflexively against hers. "No," he managed to say in a raspy tone. "I can't."

The memory of what took place after Garrick spoke those three simple words had the power to move her, causing her breath to quicken and her fingers to clench—even now, years later, as she sat alone in her office.

She had to stop, she told herself firmly as she bent again over her calendar. Daydreaming about the past was getting her nowhere.

When Elise heard the door open then close again, she didn't look up. "Listen, Pat," she said, frowning, "what would happen if I put off this meeting with Burrell until sometime in April? How ticked off do you think he would be?"

"Smile at him, little star, and he'll forgive you for anything."

When she heard the deep voice, her head jerked up. A man leaned against the door, tanned, muscular arms folded across a broad chest. The sun had added platinum streaks to his dark blond hair, making his brown eyes look even darker. Here was the kind of man who would draw a second and even third look from the women he passed on the street.

"Max?" she whispered. Jumping up from her chair, she shrieked, "*Max!*" just seconds before she hurled herself into his arms.

"Ellie? Ellie!" he mimicked, laughing when she punched him in the arm.

"What are you doing here? Never mind that, where have you been? And why the hell didn't I get a letter? Not one stinking letter from you in four years! Not a note, not a postcard, not even a message sent by jungle drums, you sadistic jerk."

Releasing her, Max moved to sit in the chair

facing her desk. Elise followed him and, rather than return to her chair, sat on the desk, swinging one crossed leg impatiently as she waited for an answer.

"I told you before I left where I was going," Max reminded her.

"You told me you were going to some little Japanese island to do a thing for *National Geographic*. Please don't try to tell me it took four years to complete one illustrated article."

"It got out of hand," he said with a careless shrug. "It's a book now."

"That's it? You disappear for four years and all you can say is 'it got out of hand'?"

She didn't know why she was surprised. Max had never done anything the conventional way. Very early in his career as a photographer, he had gained a reputation for being an unpredictable genius. When a subject captured his interest, his work was guaranteed to be spectacular. When it didn't, he might not even bother to turn in the assignment.

Leaning forward, Max picked up the nameplate from her desk and whistled through his teeth. "I'm impressed. You've come a long way from Weiden Street, kid. I knew you'd eventually get tired of modeling." He waved a careless hand at her office. "When did all this happen?"

"Right after Garrick and I married. You knew I was married now?"

"As a matter of fact, I did hear about that." He gave her a dissecting look. "Caught yourself a big fish, have you? I've seen his picture in the newspaper. A brooding Heathcliff type. He's the one who always has his hand in his pocket, like whatever's going on is interrupting his busy schedule and he's getting ready to blow the joint."

"Not Heathcliff. Mr. Rochester," she said quietly. "He keeps his hand in his pocket because it's disfigured."

A mental picture of the terrible burn scars on Garrick's left hand, scars that twisted his long fingers, rose in her mind, and pain began spreading outward from her heart.

Shaking away the emotion, she said, "His left hand was burned."

"That's too bad." Max studied her face closely. "Something that happened recently? It must be if he's still self-conscious about it."

"No, the scars look old." Her lips curved in a small, wry smile. "I don't know when or how it happened. I did ask once, but he changed the subject and—well, he closed himself off on the topic. You'd have to know him to understand what I mean."

"You asked once?" Max's disbelief was obvious. "That doesn't sound like you, Ellie. You've been married to this guy—for over two years now?—and you don't know about something that's obviously such an important part of his life?"

"I guess that's part of the reason we're separated." She glanced away from Max's penetrating gaze. "No communication. The number-one reason marriages fail."

Slipping off the desk, she walked three steps away before swinging back around toward Max. "You don't know how I hate the sound of that. I resent being a statistic. It should be more personal. We should be allowed our own special reason for failing."

After a moment he said, "I'm sorry, kid. What are you going to do?"

"I'm twenty-eight, Max." She shoved back a strand of dark hair. "I hate rocking the boat— I'm inconveniencing Garrick, and Mona wants to throttle me—but I want more from marriage. I want to be in love with a man who loves me in return."

"Don't do it," Max said, the words harsh and abrupt. "Don't love, Ellie. It'll kill you."

She moved, reaching out to stroke his face. He looked so angry . . . and so pained. "Does it still hurt?" she whispered.

He wouldn't look at her, and he didn't answer. But then he didn't need to. Although Max always played it light, Elise knew the truth. In the past ten years Max had turned into a hard man. A hard, cynical man, so different from what he used to be, back when they were all together on Weiden Street.

Back then, Elise, Max, and Annie Seaton had spent every waking hour together, and as a result Elise had been witness to the love that had grown steadily between the other two. She had been there the day their love had blazed out of control. Elise thought then that it was the most beautiful, the most moving, thing she had ever seen, and in her heart she had known that Max and Annie were made for each other. Obviously her heart had been mistaken, because three months after Max and Annie's wedding, the bride had left town with the groom's brother.

"At first I wanted to kill them both," said Max, his deep voice startling her. "Later I wanted to die myself. I actively tried to do away with myself, but not directly, not by putting a bullet through my brain. I just stepped in front of danger every chance I got." Glancing up, he met her gaze. "Never depend so completely on another human being for your happiness, Ellie. You might as well cut your throat and get it over with."

Elise hurt for him now as she had then, but she knew he couldn't possibly view the events of his life with any kind of objectivity. He couldn't step back and see that it wasn't love that had made him hard and cynical. It was the absence of love. When Annie ran out on him, Max had shut love out of his life, the same way being married to Garrick had shut love out of Elise's. And she'd be damned if she would let what happened to Max happen to her. She didn't want to become bitter. She didn't want to spend her life in a place as cold and lonely as where Max lived.

"Even if your marriage isn't perfect," he said, "I can't see you just giving up on it. That's not like you. If Fane wants to work it out—"

"He's having an affair," she said bluntly. It was the first time she had said the words aloud, and they seemed to roar through the room.

Max frowned. "You're sure?"

"Of course I'm sure." She glanced away from his steady gaze. "I even know who she is."

"Come on, Ellie, what are you not telling me?"

"Leave me alone." She heard the defensive, sulky note in her voice and hated it.

Moving to stand in front of her, he said, " 'Fess up, Ellie."

She glared at him. "You bastard. All right, all right. Several months ago I hired an investigator—Stop it. Don't you dare laugh," she said as he began to do just that. After a moment she grinned against her will. "I know, it sounds like part of the plot for a soap opera, doesn't it? But I did it, and that's all there is to it. So now I've got a dirty little file on my husband and his mistress. I have pictures of them together. And I've got background material on Charis that contradicts everything Garrick has told me about her."

Charis Hayden was the wife of Garrick's best friend, Walter. And even though for the past two-and-a-half years the two couples had met socially several times a week, Elise had never suspected a thing. Walter, apparently, had been more perceptive, because several months earlier he had suddenly left Charis. He simply walked out and moved back East. After Walter's desertion Garrick began to spend more and more time with Charis, compensating her in his own special way for the loss of her husband.

"I'm sorry, Ellie," said Max, breaking the silence. "You want me to go beat the tar out of him?"

"Silly," she said. "It didn't hurt. Which shows

how little we had left. I'm not the woman I was when we married, and he's not the same man. How can I be hurt because a *stranger* is fooling around with another woman?" She met his skeptical look. "Okay, I'm sad, but my feelings have nothing to do with Garrick. I'm sad for the love that got lost." When she smiled, her lip quivered, but only a little. "The loss of any love depletes the world's store. And that's a shame, because the world needs all it can get."

Reaching out, Max pulled her onto his lap and cradled her head gently against his shoulder. "I didn't want this for you," he murmured huskily. "I never wanted to see that particular look in your eyes."

Framing her face with his hands, he held it away from him so he could see her features. After a moment he said, "Okay, okay, I've got it. There's only one thing for you to do now. You've got to throw yourself into a meaningless affair. You and I need to get something good and hot going. Believe me, a little heavy breathing will do you a world of good."

She sputtered with laughter. "I can tell passion for me is just eating you alive."

"A man who could hold you without being aroused is a dead man, sugar. And I'm not dead yet."

Bending her over the arm of the chair, he began spreading noisy kisses, enthusiastic but lust-free, all over her face while she shook with helpless laughter.

Two

Garrick stood in the doorway, watching his wife in the arms of a stranger. What held him still was not that a stranger was kissing her. It was her laugh. He had never heard Elise laugh in that particular way. It was natural, free, almost abandoned.

Closing the door behind him, he shoved his left hand in his pocket and moved into the room. At the soft click Elise glanced up, her laughter fading in surprise.

"Garrick, what are you—Let me up, you idiot," she said to the man who held her. Her voice was unsteady with laughter.

She rose with the unconscious grace that never failed to impress Garrick. He always expected to hear music from centuries past—something elegantly erotic—playing in the background when she moved. Elise was tall and slim, her curves not the blatant centerfold kind, but subtly, elusively sensual. Green-gold eyes framed by long black lashes stood out against her creamy complexion. The delicately slanted eyes and high cheekbones in combination with her long, slender neck gave her the aristocratic look of an Egyptian princess. Her long, straight hair was cut in a dramatic style. And its deep, deep brown color reminded him of strong black coffee.

"It's good to see you," she said, then after a slight pause added, "I don't think you've met Max . . . Maximilian Decatur. Max, this is my husband, Garrick Fane."

As the men shook hands, she moved to the other side of her desk, regaining her chair. "Max is a photojournalist. You've probably seen his work."

Garrick nodded, studying the other man's features. "Don't we have a photograph of you at home, one left over from Elise's modeling days?"

When Decatur sent Elise a flagrantly vulgar gesture, she laughed. This time her laugh was the kind with which Garrick was familiar. It was husky and deftly provocative.

"I still don't know how she talked me into taking that stupid job," Max muttered.

"Max thinks there's something unnatural and not quite macho about a man posing for photographs. 'Pretty boy postulation,' he calls it."

"I take it the two of you are old friends," said Garrick, smiling.

Instantly he intercepted a look that passed

between them. When Decatur raised one brow, Elise grimaced in silent apology. Apparently this man was more than a casual friend. Which made the fact that she had never mentioned him even more mystifying.

"I met Max when I lived with my father," Elise said.

Elise rarely talked about the time she had spent with her father, which had led Garrick to believe those years had been bad ones for her. Obviously they hadn't been all bad.

Her visitor rose lazily to his feet. "Gotta run, little star."

"Don't you dare disappear again," she said, and there was a definite warning in her voice.

"Don't get your drawers in a wad. I'll call you tonight. Nice to meet you, Garrick," he said as an afterthought just before he closed the door.

As soon as Max had left the room, Elise turned her full attention to Garrick. The word that always came to mind when she looked at her husband was *control*. His black hair was precisely cut, his clothes perfectly tailored. His navy-blue eyes were dark enough to be mistaken initially for black; they were the kind of eyes that seemed capable of seeing through brick walls. Although he was taller than Max, he was not as muscular. But Elise knew, better than anyone, the strength Garrick possessed. It wasn't the showy kind, but it was as powerful and unyielding as steel.

"Little star?" he queried, raising one dark brow as he sat in the chair Max had vacated.

She winced. "An old nickname, left over from the days when I was positive I would be a movie star."

He studied her for a moment. "Starbright," he said. "It still fits."

"Oh, Lord." She laughed. "I'm glad no one else thought to put the two together. I would never have heard the end of it." She shook her head and smiled politely. "So, what are you doing in my part of town?"

"I had to see a client, and since I was in the area, I thought I'd stop by to talk to you about Mona."

She groaned, covering her face with her hands. "I'm sorry, Garrick. I had hoped she would limit her badgering to me."

"She said you finally agreed to go to her birthday party."

Dropping her hands, she sent him a speaking look. "Do you really think I had a choice?"

He laughed. "Not without a note from your doctor, and only then if you had a dangerous communicable disease."

"Or a disfiguring one. I have a feeling Mona would let me off the hook if I somehow managed to get real ugly in the next two weeks."

He shook his head. "You couldn't do that, not if you had two hundred years."

"You're sweet," she said, murmuring the words automatically as she turned toward the blinking light on her telephone. "Excuse me for a second," she said, punching the button. "Yes, Pat?"

As Pat told her about the incoming call, Elise watched Garrick from the corners of her eyes. Although the surface was as controlled as always, there seemed to be an unsettled, electric air about him.

"Tell her I'm in conference and ask her to hold for a couple of minutes," Elise said to her secretary, then turned back to her husband. "I take it you agreed to go as well."

He shrugged. "I like Mona. Besides, I can't afford to offend one of my biggest fans. That's why I dropped by. Since we're both going, we may as well take the Cessna and fly there together."

She bit her lip. "I don't know, Garrick. I was thinking of asking Max to go with me."

He nodded. "I assumed you would bring a date. I'm bringing one myself. The plane seats six," he reminded her unnecessarily.

How terribly civilized, she thought, then hitched up her shoulders in a shrug. "Sure, why not? I'll see you in a couple of weeks then." When he didn't stand immediately to leave, she said, "Was there something else you needed to talk to me about?"

Exhaling slowly, he said, "Nothing that won't keep." He got up slowly and walked to the door, leaving her to wonder about the strange look in his dark eyes.

In a wingback chair that was positioned at a slight angle to the fireplace, Elise sat with a cup of coffee cradled between her fingers. The bare flesh of her arms and the pale yellow silk of her negligee gleamed in the flickering light.

Tonight she had intended to search through her files for the perfect model to represent Good 'n Fresh Milk, someone blond and wholesome, someone who wouldn't look ridiculous hugging a cow. But seeing Max in her office, talking to him after dinner this evening, had made it impossible to concentrate. It was funny how simply seeing someone could throw her so completely into the past that she felt the way she had the last time she'd seen him. But seeing Max had done even more than that. Seeing Max had sent her all the way back to Weiden Street.

She smiled, and when she drew in a slow breath, it felt as though she were inhaling memories instead of ordinary air.

Back then, back on Weiden Street, she had had such high hopes for the future. Someday she was going to be rich and famous, she had told Max and Annie. Someday she would live in a house that didn't have bugs big enough to carry her away. She would have a yard without a single bare patch, a yard that didn't know how to grow grass burrs. And she would wear clothes with satin labels instead of stiff plastic ones.

Elise had got away from Weiden Street, just as she had sworn she would. She got away in spirit as well as in body, and the change begun in her modeling years seemed complete by the time she married Garrick. She had convinced herself that nothing remained of the unpolished, awkward girl she had been back then. But the instant she saw Max again, she knew the changes were superficial, the polish only on the surface. Inside, Elise was still unfinished material.

"Rich and famous," she murmured, a short laugh escaping her. She had achieved a satisfying amount of both wealth and fame in the years since then. Why hadn't she known, back on Weiden Street, that it wouldn't be enough?

Elise had been five when she and her father had moved to the depressingly dull housing addition in East Dallas, and she had only brief flashes of memory from the times before, when her mother and father were still together. Although she couldn't summon up a picture of how Jason and Sharon, her mother's children from her first marriage, had looked back then, she remembered the way they had either pampered or tormented her as the mood struck them.

The only memory with any strength was the memory she held of her mother screaming in anger while her father cried.

At the time Elise had no way of knowing her parents' arguments were caused by the financial problems that arose when Daniel Bright lost his cushy job at an oil company, and that her father, past fifty when Elise was born, was too close to retirement age to find another executive position. She only knew she and her father were suddenly alone.

Years later Elise learned that her mother had made an attempt to retain custody of her, a very brief attempt. Mona had relinquished her rights readily enough when new, wealthier husband material appeared on the scene. As it turned out, Albie—the new man—didn't quite like the idea of raising another man's children, so Mona gave up on her youngest daughter and sent Jason and Sharon off to boarding school.

Elise assumed she had grieved for her mother. It would have been the natural thing for a five-year-old to do. But for the life of her, she couldn't remember any feelings of loss. Looking back, it seemed to her she had instantly adjusted, becoming just another kid in the Weiden Street brat pack. They were the forerunners of the latchkey kids, making their own ways through the world surrounding Weiden Street while their parents worked.

As an adolescent, Elise—tall, thin, and painfully shy—had gravitated toward the other oddballs, the other two outcasts in her small neighborhood. Max was Weiden Street's sensitive, brilliant bad boy. He and his younger brother, Roger, lived with their aunt Charlotte in the house next door to Elise's. Roger was a born troublemaker, but in Charlotte's eyes he could do no wrong. Max, on the other hand, had been cast in the role of demon, and for reasons of his own, had chosen to live up to his reputation to the best of his considerable ability.

Annie Seaton was the other outcast. Beautiful, tormented Annie, weighed down by a mother who was a weekend prostitute. Elise could still remember the agony in Annie's eyes when the girl discovered that several members of the high school football team in a group had visited her mother one Saturday night.

Elise, Max, and Annie had spent every free moment together. They were family, taking care of one another, helping one another though the bad times. And together, they had built dreams of a better, brighter future.

Then, when she was sixteen, Elise suddenly blossomed. Overnight, it seemed, she grew into her long limbs. Although she wasn't conventionally beautiful, prom-queen pretty, she had something that made people turn to look at her and watch her until she was out of sight. Something about her eyes and the way she moved never failed to draw attention. It took only a suggestion from her home-economics teacher to set Elise on the way to turning her dreams into reality.

"Look into modeling," Miss Tripp had told her.

Elise, with her usual cast-iron determination, had done more than look into it. Max's camera and the makeup kit Annie had borrowed from her mother had transformed Elise into a beautiful, sophisticated young woman with a portfolio to rival any professional's.

Elise had been modeling locally for two years when Daniel Bright died in an accident. By that time Max and Annie were both gone from Weiden Street, and Elise was left with no one. Or so she thought. Out of the blue, Mona turned up at her ex-husband's funeral, giving her own wordy brand of comfort to her grieving daughter. Before she knew what was happening, Elise had her own room in Mona and Albie's enormous University Park home.

At the time Elise had been too stunned to question her mother's motives, to ask why she suddenly wanted to take care of her estranged daughter. Eventually, though, the desperate sense of loss began to dull and, she realized with only a small amount of heartache, that if she hadn't been a model, Mona most likely would have decided Elise was old enough to take care of herself.

Her sojourn at her mother's home lasted for a little more than a year. Mona had divorced Albie by that time, which meant there was a steady flow of new candidates through the house. Jason and Sharon, both grown and married, were constantly at the house, and when they weren't fighting with each other, they turned their antagonism toward Elise. Trish was even worse. The product of Mona's union with Albie was a young teenager who couldn't abide the sight of her half-sister. In every direction Elise turned, a new war was erupting, so she packed her bags and moved to New York. It was time, she had convinced herself, to take a shot at the toughest, most exciting city in the world.

Her luck held. Within three years no model was more in demand than Elise Adler Bright. Her look of cool, sophisticated sensuality had worked well for her. But, of course, it was only an act. An act that even Garrick had bought.

Looking back, Elise realized she and Garrick

had met in an artificial environment. She was the creation of makeup artists and fashion designers. Garrick had been attracted by the image she had projected, not by the real Elise, but once her role had been established, she didn't know how to say, "This isn't me. This is a woman someone made up." And if she was to be totally honest with herself, Elise knew she had been too dazzled by the way Garrick made her feel to think about whether or not their relationship was based in reality.

Their first week together, that magical week after they met, had been followed by a month of telephone calls and quick flights between Dallas and New York. When Garrick asked her to marry him, she hadn't even hesitated before accepting.

They had had a perfect wedding and bought the perfect house; Elise laid the groundwork for a perfect business and became the perfect hostess for their perfect social life. It was the perfect marriage for the perfect couple.

Then, during their second year together, Elise began to understand that something was missing from the perfect picture. Elise was missing. Another woman, a perfect, artificial woman, was living her life. She looked up one day and discovered everything, even her marriage, was a mockup. She was living a storyboard life.

Did I devote so much time and energy to work because I had nothing at home, or did I have nothing at home because I devoted so much time and energy to work?

Giving her head a restless shake, she leaned it

against the back of the chair. Even now, she wasn't altogether sure where she had gone wrong. She only knew she and Garrick had lost whatever they had had in the beginning. And the moment she had acknowledged that fact, the throat-closing attacks of loneliness began. She would lie in bed beside a man she didn't really know, and she would feel there was someone somewhere waiting for her, someone waiting to love her, someone waiting joyously to receive her love. As the days passed, the sensation had grown stronger and stronger until it became almost a physical presence beside her. She felt it now, as she sat all alone by the fire. She felt the waiting love reaching out to her.

"I miss you," she whispered to the emptiness. "I've missed you all my life."

Swallowing with difficulty, she shook the loneliness away, lecturing herself, as she had dozens of times before, that she was indulging in adolescent daydreams. But no matter how often she told herself it was fantasy, it still felt real. And the more her relationship with Garrick had deteriorated, the more real the sensation had become.

For months Elise had vacillated, unable or unwilling to deal with either the new feelings or the old insecurities and doubts. Then Walter Hayden had forced the issue into the open. Six months earlier Garrick's best friend had changed not one but four lives, simply by walking out on his wife.

Walter was good-natured, outgoing, and occasionally loudmouthed. He was the direct opposite of Garrick, but since the day they met at Harvard Law, they had been best friends. And because the Hayden house was only two blocks away, Elise and Garrick saw the couple frequently.

Although Elise had never given any intensive thought to the Haydens' relationship, if anyone had asked her, she would have said Walter and Charis were a model couple. They had been constantly kissing, constantly touching. They even had little pet names for each other.

"Too cute for words," muttered Elise, placing her empty coffee cup on a low table. "Too cute to be real."

Charis, a totally feminine woman, had peachy-blond hair and a lightly freckled nose. She was short and almost but not quite plump, the kind of woman men usually called a nice armful. Her pale blue eyes were habitually wide, as though she were constantly awed by the world. Charis wouldn't have looked at all ridiculous hugging a cow.

Given their husbands' relationship, the two women should have become close friends, but it didn't happen. Charis was involved in charity work, and Elise was busy with her model agency, so neither had time for doing "woman things" together. And if the truth were known, there was no inclination on either side toward friendship. They were poles apart, intellectually and philosophically. But for all that, they had been friendly. At least until the day Walter had walked out.

Walter had kept his plans to himself; he hadn't even called his best friend, an oversight that had bewildered Elise at the time. He had simply packed his bags and left. But Charis had called Walter's best friend. And called and called and called.

Garrick began canceling social, and even business, engagements so he could be with Charis. His explanation was that since Charis was an only child whose parents were both deceased, she had no one else to turn to.

"Lies, all lies," Elise said softly to the fire.

The investigator she had hired had found Charis's parents living in Fort Worth, and Charis's older sister had an apartment not ten miles from the Hayden house. Elise assumed Garrick had told the lie so his wife wouldn't question the amount of time he was spending with the blond.

On the rare occasions that Garrick wasn't with Charis, the woman would call Elise to find out where Garrick was. It was during one of those telephone conversations that Elise learned of her husband's affair.

"He's not here, Charis," Elise had said, keeping her voice polite but cool. Garrick had been in New York for several days on business and wasn't due back until that evening. "Is there something I can do for you?"

"I need *Garrick*. I've got to talk to Garrick." As usual, Charis sounded on the verge of hysteria. "I've called his office, but he's not there. I don't understand it . . . he left here over an hour ago. He's had plenty of time to get to his office by now."

Elise felt a moment of inexplicable nausea. "He left your house an hour ago?" she said through dry lips.

"A little over an hour. And I didn't even get a chance to talk to him this morning. He overslept, and there wasn't time. Where can he be, Elise? I've got to find him. I'm about to go crazy. You wouldn't believe—"

Elise had gently replaced the receiver, welcoming the numbness that spread through her body and mind. When Garrick came home that night, Elise hadn't met him with anger. There were ground rules in their marriage—and making nasty accusations while throwing the expensive bric-a-brac certainly violated those rules. She had calmly asked how his trip went. With equal calm he had told her all about it. He spoke about his meeting with his new client, about the play he had seen, and about the new dessert he had sampled at their favorite Manhattan restaurant.

As he was loosening his tie on his way to shower and change for dinner, he had mentioned casually, as though it were an insignificant detail, that Charis was having problems, so he came back early to deal with them. He didn't bother to mention he had come back a whole day early; he didn't bother to mention where he had spent the night; and he didn't bother to explain how the hell Charis had known how to get in touch with him in New York.

And Elise hadn't asked. She had simply let it go. But something had happened to her that night. There was a feeling deep inside her, some unnamed, unsettling emotion she couldn't look at. As soon as she tried to find it and analyze it, it disappeared into inertia.

It wasn't the last time Garrick had spent stolen time with Charis. Too many nights Elise had smelled the other woman's perfume on him. Too many nights he had called with a feeble excuse for being late.

Hearing his lies, knowing he was sleeping with Charis, had clarified things for Elise. On some level she had already known that their marriage was over, but she had done nothing about it. She had been waiting for something solid, something she could point to and say, "There it is. That's where it ended."

Three months before, when she had explained to Garrick that she wanted a separation, there had been no fireworks, no arguments, no demands for an explanation. For a long time he hadn't said anything at all. He had stood by the fireplace, his back to her, his left hand in his pocket.

Finally he turned to face her, and after saying he respected her decision, he told her if she wanted a legal separation, he could find someone competent to handle it for her, someone who would look out for her interests.

Elise didn't know what she had expected. A little regret maybe. A little anger. But she had known that however he handled it, the scene would be civilized, because above all Garrick was a civilized man.

"So civilized. So bloody, damned civilized," she said as she rested the back of her head against the chair. The retrospection had left her drained but strangely calm. Too calm.

There should be an empty whiskey bottle on the table, she told herself with a small, sad smile. There should have been some signs of distress on her part. The death of a marriage should have been attended by a mournful dirge, by weeping and wailing, by the pulling of hair and the beating of breasts. By *something*.

Elise had told Max she was sad because of the loss of love, but she was even sadder that the loss should cause so little notice.

Three

Garrick sat in his car, leaning one arm against the steering wheel as he stared at the house. For the past hour he had been staring at the house, recalling events in his life, thinking of the changes and traumas he had had to face. He'd remembered the times he had managed to handle those changes and traumas well. The times he hadn't.

He couldn't sit there all night. *Get out and get it over with*, he told himself.

Elise opened the door only moments after he rang the bell. "Garrick, you idiot," she said, smiling. "You don't have to use the doorbell. You can just come on in, it's your home, too."

The look in her eyes contradicted her words. She was not pleased to see him, he realized, and the hand in his pocket clenched into a fist in reaction.

She was wearing the yellow silk pajamas he had bought for her during a business trip in San Francisco. As always, she looked beautiful and poised. Untouchable. Unreachable.

Following her into the den, Garrick stood by the door and glanced around the room. It was the first time he had been back since they had separated. The room seemed perfect, as did the rest of the house, but he had always felt something was a bit off, and he had never been able to put his finger on it. Was it all just a little too perfect?

Garrick hadn't said a word since he had entered the house, and although he had never been a garrulous man, his continued silence made Elise nervous and, somehow, defensive. He was still in the strange, restive mood she had noticed in her office earlier.

"Come sit by the fire," she said. "It's a little chilly out tonight. Would you like a cup of coffee?"

Only after she had brought his coffee and freshened her own did he take the chair on the other side of the fireplace. He sat for a while drinking the coffee as he stared into the flames before glancing up to catch her eye.

"It's been some time since we separated," he said quietly. "I thought maybe we should talk about the next step."

Was Charis pushing for marriage? Elise wondered. According to the investigator, Garrick was only the most recent in a long string of affairs for Charis. For a moment Elise was tempted to warn her husband about his new love—she didn't like the idea of his being in Walter's position at some point in the future—but she immediately suppressed the urge. Garrick was well able to take care of himself.

Glancing up, she found him studying her face and realized he was waiting for a response from her. "Yes, I guess you're right," she said. "You're the legal expert. What do you suggest?"

"A marriage counselor," he replied immediately. "I've checked into it and have a list for you to look at. You could give each of them a call and see which one you think you could work with."

She frowned. "I don't know, Garrick. I mean, I realize it's the done thing . . . it's what our friends would expect from us next, but I thought a legal separation would—oh, I don't know. Maybe I believed it would serve the same purpose for us."

His dark brows drew together. "The same purpose? What exactly was the separation supposed to accomplish?"

"I knew I couldn't simply file for divorce." She moistened her lips as the unexpected tension between them increased. "That's too . . . too blunt. Too crude. People would assume something ugly had happened between us. I didn't want that. I didn't want to embarrass you in any way." Throwing him a questioning look, she added, "Would seeing a counselor help you save face?"

"Actually, I wasn't suggesting it for the benefit of our friends or my face," he said, his tone dry. "I thought it might get us to the point of reconciliation."

It was Elise's turn to study Garrick. What kind of game was he playing now? Was he making a pretense of trying to keep their marriage together because it would make a good story to tell at the country club, because it might stir up some sympathy for him? He could tell his friends he had begged her to try to work it out, but she had hardened her heart against him.

That kind of pettiness didn't sound like Garrick, but on the other hand, Elise was very popular with her husband's friends and business associates. Maybe he was afraid they would give Charis a hard time if it became known that the breakup was partly her fault. If he could play the cast-off husband who had turned to Charis for comfort, everyone, except Elise, of course, would come off looking good.

She gave a slight shake of her head. It wasn't necessary to know what motivated Garrick's suggestion. She would go on as she had begun, playing out the farce until it was finally over.

"I don't think so, Garrick," she said quietly. "That would only drag it out. We have to admit to ourselves—believe me, I know how difficult it is—but we have to admit we failed. Do you realize we've never had an argument? Not a real one. We've never even raised our voices in anger." She shook her head restlessly. "That's a

pretty good clue that something's wrong somewhere."

Rising abruptly to his feet, he shoved his
hand into his pocket and walked to stand before
the fireplace. "You want to divorce me because I
didn't yell at you?"

Was this part of the game? And if it was, how
was she supposed to react? What were her
lines? Was she supposed to forget the times she
had seen, deep in his dark eyes, the barely
suppressed emotion, some powerful yet banked
force? His anger or frustration or rage, whatever
it was, had been kept carefully away from her,
away from the person who should have been
sharing it with him. Never, not once, had he
allowed the dark side of his nature to surface.
Elise had known for a long time that something
explosive was at work inside him, but she had
never been permitted to get close enough to him
to identify its source.

Drawing in a slow breath, she reminded herself she had only to stay calm for a little while
longer. Just a little while longer.

"I'm not blaming you," she said carefully. "I'm
not even talking about you. I'm talking about us
as a couple. Something subtle but absolutely
necessary was missing between us. It threw our
relationship off kilter. That one missing ingre-
dient made everything else wrong."

He moved toward her with measured steps,
and when he stood close beside her, he gazed
down at her, his strong lips twisting in a strange
smile.

"Everything, Elise?" Reaching out, he pushed her hair behind one ear with the light brush of a finger. "Everything?"

Elise began reacting to his touch, to his nearness, even before he pulled her to her feet. She was both wary and aware, and to her regret, more aware than wary. It was always the same. This immediate, mutual fascination was the thing that had drawn them together in the first place. Prudence was tossed to the wind the moment he touched her.

"It's been a long time," he murmured, his deep voice husky. "Too long, Elise."

Much, much too long, she agreed silently. She wanted him badly. She had a deep hunger for the things he did to her. She needed to feel again all those feelings only he could draw out of her.

When the hoarse sound of pleasure escaped him, she knew he had recognized her response. Of course he'd recognized it, she told herself. When had she ever been able to hide it from him? As his strong lips closed over hers, his right hand pushed its way beneath the layers of silk to find her breast. And, as always, his touch was agonizingly beautiful. Garrick was an expert at awakening her hunger. With no apparent effort, he could make her throb with tormenting sensations all the way to her bones.

As wave after wave of heart-shaking desire swept through her, she sensed that her knees were about to give way. Garrick moved with her as he began to lower her to the floor.

It couldn't happen. *It could not happen.*

Elise moaned into his open mouth, fighting against the overpowering emotions as she had never fought against anything in her life. In an act of sheer desperation she conjured up a picture of Charis, a picture of Charis and Garrick together, a picture of Garrick lowering Charis to the floor.

"No." She groaned and pulled frantically away from him and stood.

With unsteady steps she moved to grasp the chair back, using it to hold herself upright, and for long moments she heard only the hoarse, raspy sound of her own breathing, unbelievably loud in the quiet room. Then, finally, mercifully, she began to regain some measure of control.

"Old—" She broke off and cleared her throat. "Old habits die hard. Especially habits that are as addictive as that one." She turned around slowly to face her husband. "As you so effectively pointed out a few minutes ago, not everything was wrong. But as wonderful as making love with you has always been, as much as I want you now, it's not enough." Her voice was filled with gentle regret. "You can base an affair on sex, Garrick, but not a lifetime commitment."

He stood perfectly still, his features looking as if they'd been chiseled from stone. He didn't move or speak for so long that Elise's fingers clenched in nervous reaction.

At last he shrugged his shoulders, gingerly, as though they were bruised and sore. "No." The word sounded abrupt and harsh. "No, I guess not."

When he turned to go, the emotion in his eyes confused her. He looked lost and lonely. So damned lonely. Almost, almost she asked him to stay the night with her. She had to bite her lip to hold back the words. It wouldn't help anything. Maybe Garrick was as sad about the failure of their marriage, about the loss of their love, as she was. They both had to let go. The only thing they could do now was walk into the future with the knowledge of the past to guide them. They had to guard against making the same mistakes again.

But hadn't she already admitted that she wasn't sure where she had gone wrong? Did Garrick know? How could either of them know anything when they had never really talked? And maybe that was their biggest failure of all.

"Garrick?"

When she spoke, he paused, but didn't look back.

"Next time," she said slowly, "I mean, when you find someone you think you could care for, talk to her. Don't hold back parts of yourself. Share what's inside you with her."

Still without turning, he said, "Good advice, Elise. Just make sure you apply it to yourself as well."

He didn't have to worry about that, she thought as she heard the front door close. When she found the one who was waiting to love her, Elise would give him everything. He would know every inch of her mind and heart and soul . . . not just her body. Because to the one who loved her, she would be able to give nothing less than all she had.

Garrick gripped the steering wheel with both hands, his shoulders tense, his neck stiff, as he headed back to the hotel where he had been staying since their separation. Seconds later, in a purely instinctive move, he swerved across two lanes, bringing belligerent responses from several late-night travelers. Then he found the freeway exit and turned onto it.

He wasn't ready to face an empty hotel suite. He couldn't find one good reason why he should go back there where nothing and no one waited for him.

He drove aimlessly for a quarter of an hour, wandering through a part of town that was unfamiliar to him. And from the looks of it, it wasn't an area he particularly wanted to become familiar with. Except for two or three run-down clubs, their neon signs wearily beckoning non-existent customers, the street was lined with dark, low buildings, all of them built before the word *skyscraper* had even been invented.

Pulling over to the side of the street, he parked and locked his car, pocketing the keys as he stepped onto the uneven, narrow sidewalk. He had no destination in mind. He simply needed to walk.

Being with Elise tonight had left him restless, flooded with all-too-familiar emotions. Anger.

Resentment. Bitterness. And as always, a gut-wrenching, soul-deep need.

In the past few months, during countless sleepless nights, Garrick had relived every moment of their marriage, twisting and turning in an alien bed, torturing himself with pictures from the past. Tonight the thought of the long night ahead was unbearable.

He would keep walking until he felt human again. Until the sight and sound and scent of her left him. Until he could no longer feel her hair on his face, her firm breasts beneath his fingers. Until the essence of her faded from his heart, setting him free.

Free? The thought made him laugh aloud, and the sound was unnaturally loud in the dark street, causing a passing drunk to wave and echo the laugh.

Did he really think he would ever be free of her? Even if he could go back to the very beginning, knowing what he knew now, it would make no difference. There had never been any alternative. It had been written down in some twisted god's book that she would be his obsession. That he would be eternally blinded by her fire.

And, in truth, did he honestly want to be free? he asked himself as a fine mist began to fall. If he could wipe out every minute he had spent with her, if he could erase the way she looked when she laughed, the warmth of her body when they made early morning love, if he could eliminate every trace of her from his memory, would he do it?

He wouldn't. Because if the pieces of him that were devoted specifically to wanting Elise were cut away, there would be nothing left of him. Garrick Hewitt Fane would cease to exist.

Reaching up to rub the sore muscles in his neck, he wondered when, during their two-plus years of marriage, he had begun to resent her, resent his need for her. The resentment hadn't been there in the beginning, even though he knew she didn't love him, would never love him as he loved her. In the beginning there had been only the wonder of at last finding the woman who fit his needs so completely, a woman whose existence he had come to doubt.

Was it only three years ago? The time before Elise seemed a whole life away.

The day he had met Elise, Garrick had only recently arrived in New York on business, his mission to see a new client, Edward Frost, an eighty-year-old man who had been arrested for attacking his thirty-year-old nephew.

Early in his career, Garrick had gained his reputation because of a sensational murder case. Although he didn't like being in the public eye, he recognized the power of notoriety, how it brought in important cases—not important in the sense that they were publicized, or paid off in fat fees. Notoriety brought him cases that would be the first step in changing unfair laws. Cases that would make a difference. It was his way of fighting for what he believed in. The Frost case was something he believed in.

After Frost's arrest, the old man's nephew had asked the courts to declare his uncle unfit to stand trial. He agreed not to press charges if Edward Frost would go into a hospital for treatment of a mental disorder.

Within minutes of meeting the elderly man, Garrick had been convinced he was perfectly sane. He was stubborn and disagreeable, sometimes downright nasty, but not crazy. Mr. Frost, with surprising belligerence, declared it was his constitutional right to go to jail for attacking his nephew. He had done it, he said, and he was glad he had done it, and he was perfectly willing to pay for his crime. But the old man's pride was at stake, and he couldn't abide the thought of being declared incompetent, of seeing his nephew gain control of his small estate.

Garrick had to show that Edward Frost wasn't mentally unstable, just mean. Garrick had had no doubt he would win in the jury trail. He understood the old man and felt qualified to interpret his feelings and actions to the court.

That day, the day he had met Elise, when Garrick returned to his hotel, his mind had been on his recent meeting with his new client, and for a moment he thought he had wandered into the wrong building. In the four hours he had been away, someone had moved a jungle into the lobby. Banana trees—complete with bananas—ferns, stands of bamboo, a couple of monkeys, and a full-grown live cheetah were arranged around the elaborate red velvet settees.

Then he had seen her.

Even at the first moment he looked at her, he knew it wasn't her extraordinary beauty knocking him off his feet. It was the way she gazed at him, as though she saw only him, as though she had been waiting all her life for the moment she would finally see him. The awareness between them, the instant empathy, rocked through him, bringing a burst of joy so intense, so poignantly sweet, it almost devastated him.

It was the strangest sensation. He felt as though they were connected not just emotionally but physically . . . as though her blood were flowing through his veins, her thoughts running through his mind, her feelings strengthening his body.

Incredibly, taking her into himself, absorbing the essence of her across the distance, didn't in any way dilute his own personality. He became more himself than he had ever been, ever hoped to be. Looking at her, he finally knew exactly who Garrick Fane was.

For a week, one beautiful week, he had lived with the idea he had found something extraordinary, something bordering on perfection. Garrick had never believed in fairy tales, and he had given up believing in miracles when his sister died. But he came to believe that, without looking for it, he had stumbled across a magical woman.

He believed it until the first time they had

made love. He believed until the moment she closed her eyes when he touched her.

Garrick had been only twenty when his hand was burned, a young man with his fair share of the optimism of youth. And he had never been a vain man, not before and certainly not after the accident. He felt justified in assuming he would be accepted for what he was inside.

After all, he could still use the hand, he had told himself, and at least he was alive. The plastic surgeons who worked on his hand had done what they could, and Garrick had been satisfied with their efforts.

Then he saw the way his parents reacted to the scars. That was when he began pulling inside himself. That was when he began watching, noticing other people's reaction to him, especially the women he dated. He saw them pretending not to look at his hand, pretending not to shudder when it brushed against them. The coming of age that had begun with his sister's death was completed by careless people.

The truth, like most truths, was painful, but Garrick had adjusted. He accepted the fact that there were people in the world, including his own parents, who were disgusted and repelled by imperfection.

Cynicism made him stronger. Strong enough, he thought, to stand alone. But then he found Elise. And he convinced himself that with her, it would be different. The magnitude of what he had felt that day in a New York hotel lobby had made him believe Elise would accept him, all parts of him, even his disfigured hand.

On their first night together, when he had learned the truth, when he saw her close her eyes to shut out the sight of him, something fragile, something that had only just begun to grow inside him, shriveled and died, leaving a bitter pain around his heart.

When Elise closed her eyes, she couldn't see him, she couldn't see his scarred hand. And she always closed her eyes. Always.

After a while he began to wonder who she saw when her eyes were closed. Who did she pretend he was when she shut him out?

He should have broken it off then. He should have got as far away from her as possible. But he couldn't. Even knowing how she felt about him, he still couldn't stay away from her. He needed her too badly.

Bitterness boiled inside him, twisting him, but eventually, inevitably, he had decided that he would take her any way he could get her. She wanted him just as badly as he wanted her, and if she preferred an anonymous touch in the dark, he would give her that. His wife would never be deprived. Elise would have the best sex life of any woman in the state of Texas. He would see to it.

After their wedding, Elise had adjusted well, playing the part of devoted wife to perfection, and sometimes Garrick almost fooled himself into believing that they were the perfect, loving couple everyone believed them to be. Then, during the second year of their marriage, everything changed. Although mistakes were made on both sides, those mistakes were only symptoms of the deeper trouble between them, a gap that grew wider and deeper with each passing day.

The desire between them was as strong as ever—perhaps even stronger—but suddenly it wasn't enough for her. She wanted out.

Damn her soul, she wanted out.

Hours later, when Garrick walked into his hotel suite, he didn't bother with the lights. Loosening his tie, he walked across the room and pulled the drapes to expose a glass wall, letting the night lights of the city into the room with him. After removing his damp jacket, he turned a small armchair around to face the wall, poured himself a drink, and slumped down in the chair.

On his walk in the light rain that had come in the wake of a fine mist, Garrick had called up the disillusionment and the bitterness that wove in and out of his relationship with Elise. Those were the memories that were easiest to deal with.

Now, as he sat staring into space, he brought up other memories, the ones that made his nights a living hell. He saw her lying naked in his bed, her body glistening with the heat of desire, desire he knew without a doubt only his kiss, only his touch, could inspire. He heard too many times the husky words, words holding truth, her voice telling him that no one could make her come alive as he did. And her body echoed the words, moving beneath his lips, reveling in the feel of his tongue, his lips, and his body.

Sitting in the dark, he gave himself over to the memories, and when the first rays of the sun appeared in the east, spilling over and around the tall buildings, turning Dallas into a city of gold, he was still slumped in the chair, still staring out the window, still drinking.

The long night, the battle he had fought in the darkness, had anesthetized his emotions, bringing a peace of sorts, and with peace came a decision.

She thought it was over. She thought she could end this little episode in her life and go on to something else, as though nothing of any importance had happened between them.

Well, she was wrong. It wasn't over. It would never be over.

If he needed to fight, he would fight. If in the end they came to hate each other, he could handle it. If he had to follow her down to hell and drag her every step of the way back, he would do it.

But he would never let her go.

Four

Elise drummed her fingers impatiently on the steering wheel, waiting for yet another traffic light to turn green. This is stupid, she told herself for the thousandth time. This is so incredibly stupid.

For two weeks, since the moment she had agreed to travel to Mona's party with Garrick and his "date," Elise had been regretting her decision. She had been digging around in her psyche, trying to figure out what in sweet heaven she thought she was doing. While she didn't want antipathy to exist between herself and Garrick, was it really necessary that she pal around with him and his girlfriend? What exactly was she trying to prove, and to whom was she trying to prove it?

But it was too late to back out now. Two weeks too late. Max was waiting for her to pick him up.

Garrick and Charis were probably already on their way to the airport.

Garrick and Charis.

After a moment she relaxed her grip on the steering wheel and flexed her bloodless fingers. She would have to make an effort to get used to hearing those two names joined.

What she was feeling now, the sensation that the world was just slightly off center, was nothing more than the lingering remnants of a habit. It was like selling a house. Even if a person had outgrown the house, she couldn't stop thinking of it as hers for a long time. She'd find herself resentful, even outraged perhaps, when the new owners ripped out the lovingly tended daisies and replaced them with shrubbery.

Time would take care of any leftover possessiveness she might be feeling now, Elise assured herself firmly as the signal light finally turned green.

After passing Loop 12, she began looking for Bobo's Fried Chicken and Catfish, which, according to Max, was next door to and slightly to the front of his current residence. When she spotted the sprawling, grimy restaurant and the pink stucco motel behind it, her lips twitched. Dear, demented Max, she thought as she pulled her white Mercedes into the parking lot: Leave it to him to choose the tackiest place in town.

Driving slowly, she checked the numbers on the faded brown doors, and minutes later pulled into the space in front of number 27, but before she could turn off the engine, Max came out carrying a dark blue duffel bag.

As he slid into the seat beside her, Elise stared at him and slowly shook her head. "This place is a real gem, you know that? It must have taken you days to find a motel this cruddy. Why do you always stay in places I'm afraid to set foot in, even in broad daylight? And don't try to tell me this is all you can afford. Those stark little pictures of yours bring in a small fortune."

He glanced over his shoulder. "What have you got against the Palms? It has character, and so do the people who stay here. Really interesting faces. If I stayed in some high-class hotel, I wouldn't see anything but people from the other end of the ladder, the top end, people who spend a fortune trying to get rid of what experience has added to their faces—all so they can end up looking like a blank page. The folks here at the Palms have life written all over them." As she pulled out of the small parking lot, he added, "You look very uptown today."

She raised one slender brow. "I hope that's a non sequitur. Or are you putting me on the side of the blank pages?"

"Idiot. I could spend a couple of years photographing you and never catch all your expressions. I was talking about the sleek little cat suit you're wearing. Very appropriate with your green cat's eyes."

Resting one hand on her thigh, she smoothed her fingers over the roughly woven silk of her teal-blue jumpsuit. "I wore it for Mona. Mommie

Dearest would be much happier if I were still modeling, but since I'm not going to go quite that far to please her, I 'dress to impress' as a sort of consolation prize."

"Yeah, sure."

"What's that tone for? What did I say?"

"Everybody gets decked out in their sexiest clothes to impress their mamas," he said. "And the estranged husband doesn't have anything to do with it. I believe you. Sure I do. You never did explain why we're double-dating with Garrick and his little chickadee." When he paused, she could feel his gaze on her, dissecting her. "Don't try to kid me, Ellie. You may look all New York action, but inside you're still Weiden Street. You're not cut out for sophisticated games."

She opened her mouth to make excuses, then abruptly changed her mind, shaking her head helplessly instead. "No, you're right. I don't mean your implication that I made an effort to look sexy so Garrick would see what he's missing, but about my not playing sophisticated games. And I don't know why I agreed to this. I honestly don't know."

After a moment of silence Max said, "You told me two weeks ago in your office there's nothing left between you and Garrick. Since then I've seen you probably five times, and talked to you on the phone almost every night. Do you know how often you mention his name? Even when we go off on marathon talking excursions about the good old days, you manage to find a way to get Garrick into the conversation."

She frowned. "What's your point? Why are you making a big deal out of it. Garrick is one of the most intelligent people I know. Why shouldn't I quote him and . . . well, you know, repeat his opinions and conclusions? Would you stop looking at me like that?" she demanded in exasperation.

He laughed. "You're watching traffic. How do you know how I'm looking at you?"

"I can feel your keen, analytical gaze," she said dryly as she turned into the airport entrance. "And if you don't stop, I'll tell everyone how you dreamed up that particular look to intimidate Mr. Juarez into giving you a good grade on your English composition."

The Red Oak strip, as the airport was known locally, was a small airfield catering to private planes. On the weekends it was always swarming with recreational flyers, but on this day there were only a few executive types around.

Swinging the Mercedes in a wide circle, Elise parked at the rear of the squat metal hangar that housed Garrick's Cessna. She and Max had stepped out of the car and were in the process of unloading her bags from the trunk when Garrick's car pulled into the parking lot and parked several spaces away. His car was larger than Elise's, but it was in the same shade of pearl white.

Paying no attention to Max's muttered, "Mama and Daddy Mercedes? What are you trying to do, breed them?" Elise focused all her attention on the woman Garrick was at that moment helping from his car. It was the first time she had seen Charis for months.

At five-eight, Elise was comparatively short for a model, but beside Charis she felt like a giraffe. Even with the added inches the blond's ridiculously high heels gave her, Charis couldn't have been more than five-three. Today she wore a pale pink suit, expertly fashioned of lightweight wool, and a matching pink hat.

A hat, for Pete's sake, Elise thought, mentally rolling her eyes. As if Charis were on her way to meet the queen of England or something. Mona would appreciate the gesture.

When she heard Max give a soft whistle, Elise turned to him and smiled. "Remarkable, isn't she?"

"Remarkable," he agreed, slowly shaking his head. After a moment he met Elise's gaze. "Something's wrong here. No man in his right mind would go to her when he had someone like you waiting at home. The woman's a pussy willow, for Pete's sake. At a glance, a moron could tell there's no backbone to her. No grit."

Elise smiled. "Thanks . . . I think . . . but I have a feeling there's not a tremendous demand for gritty women this year." Exhaling noisily, she stooped to lift her makeup case from the trunk of the car. "I really wish you would stop blaming everything on Garrick. I told you he didn't start seeing Charis until I gave up on our marriage. And frankly, who Garrick chooses to spend his time with is his own business. Not yours. Not mine."

After a moment Max shrugged. "You sound like you're talking from a nice safe distance. Good trick if you can pull it off, and I hope you can, because I would hate like hell to see you get hurt."

She could have told Max not to worry. She had spent the last two years standing at a safe distance from her life. There was enough of that perfect, false woman left in her to play the sophisticate, enough left to smile and be polite to her husband's mistress. She even managed to be faintly amused when Garrick introduced his date to hers. It was only when Charis finally spoke to her that Elise's eight-by-ten-glossy facade slipped a little.

"Hello, Elise," the blond said softly. "How are you?"

It was a simple question. The attitude behind it, however, was a bit more complicated. Charis's expression held deference, concern, and—the low blow—a touch of compassion.

Elise's smile acknowledged the hit. "I'm fine, Charis. And you?"

Charis glanced down at the white gloves she held in one hand. "Much better, thank you." She raised her head timidly to meet Elise's gaze. "I'm so glad you agreed to come. I've been worried about you."

Elise stared at her for a moment, one brow raised. "Aren't you sweet," she murmured finally.

Garrick, his left hand in his pocket, stood next to Charis, but he seemed to have disassociated himself from the blond, from them all. It was so familiar to Elise. She had seen him so many times surrounded by people, the center of everyone's attention, but one look at his face would tell any sensitive soul that he didn't feel a part of the crowd. He had the ability to disconnect himself emotionally, to pull inside himself, so that he seemed to stand apart and above everyone else.

"As soon as I take care of the preflight inspection, we can get started."

Garrick's voice brought Elise back to her surroundings, and she realized both men were moving toward the hangar, leaving her alone with Charis. A moment of silence, a long, awkward moment, passed between the two women. Elise cleared her throat, searching her brain for something intelligent, though innocuous to say. But when the blond turned back to Elise, the words died in her throat.

Charis looked scared to death—as though she were about to be interrogated by the Gestapo. Elise didn't know whether she should feel insulted or pleased.

Swallowing a laugh, she said, "Relax, silly. Do you think I'm going to turn into a witch just because there are no witnesses? I promise I won't be tempted to scratch or bite or pull a single hair."

Charis blushed bright red. "You must hate me," she said, and it was the first time Elise had seen anyone actually wring her hands. "I tried to tell Garrick this was a mistake, but he didn't understand. He has total faith in you. He thinks you can handle anything. I just didn't know how to tell him that *I* couldn't handle it. I can't—I don't do well in tense situations." She glanced down at her hands. "I know you blame me for the breakup of your marriage, and I can't stand it when people don't like me."

"I don't blame you," Elise said slowly. "Our marriage was over long before Garrick started spending time with you."

"Really? You're not just saying that to be polite?"

She laughed. "I'm afraid I'm not as civilized as Garrick. If I blamed you . . . if I thought you were responsible for my marriage falling apart, believe me, I wouldn't be standing here talking to you."

Elise didn't see it coming and so had no chance to avoid it. Before she knew what was happening, Charis had thrown her arms around her and was hugging her.

"I'm so glad," the blond said in a breathy voice. "I've always wanted us to be friends. Maybe on this trip we can get to know each other."

Elise stood dumbstruck as Charis left to join the men. "She wants to be friends," she said slowly under her breath. "Holy hell, my husband's mistress wants to be friends. This"—she drew in a deep breath—"is going to be a very interesting trip."

Max and Charis had already taken their seats in the Cessna while Garrick stood by the cockpit and watched Elise approach. She held a small, gold-wrapped package in her hands. Today her hair was pulled back in a neat little twist at the base of her neck. It was as simple and elegant a style as the blue jumpsuit molding the sleek lines of her body and leaving her smooth back bare to the waist.

After almost three years with her he should have begun to take Elise's looks for granted. Unfortunately, that wasn't the case. Every time he looked at her, he felt his muscles tighten and his senses leap.

As he watched her walking toward him, Garrick was reminded of an exquisite piece of art, the kind found only in museums, the kind that stirred the emotions from a discreet distance. Touching it wasn't allowed. And even if a person managed to get past the barriers and the guards, he would find it cold—because it could only pull up emotions in others. It wasn't capable of giving anything in return.

No, that wasn't fair, he told himself. In bed— sweet heaven, in bed she was more open, giving, and warm than anyone he had ever met. But she saved that side of herself for the bedroom. Outside it, she once again became the untouchable, unreachable work of art.

When she drew nearer, he nodded toward the gift in her hands. "Something tastefully expensive, I assume."

"Of course," she said. "She called last week to tell me what to buy and where to buy it. Have to keep up appearances, you know. She even told me what to put on the card . . . and to sign both our names to it. I hope you don't mind."

He shook his head, irritated by the polite chitchat. "I'll give her my gift in private. Did you take a tranquilizer?" he asked as she moved past him, referring to the fact that flying in small planes had always made her nervous.

Something in his voice, some hint of the anger simmering inside him, must have reached her, surprising her. She paused and turned to look at him, a slight frown creasing her smooth brow.

"Not this time," she said slowly, then made a visible effort to regain her distant civility. "Not even a glass of sherry. I've come up with a new method. Deep breathing. I'll either relax or hyperventilate. Either way I get my mind off the fact that I'm miles above the earth in an oversized kite."

"Don't worry," he said, his voice mocking. "I promise I'll get you to Springfield, safe and sound."

She met his gaze with a silent question that had nothing to do with the words passing between them.

"I don't doubt it," she said finally. "Now if you could just guarantee my safety, mental and physical, while I'm in Mona's house, you'd have accomplished what others haven't even dared."

"I'm afraid you're on your own with your mother," he said slowly as his mind wandered away from the conversation.

Even standing before the heat of his unconcealed animosity, she managed to remain poised, and the light, teasing tone of her voice made him want to shake her. She was using her Gracious Hostess manners, wearing the face she showed to people who were acquaintances rather than friends.

Maybe hers was the most logical way to treat cast-off husbands, he told himself with mocking humor. Maybe it was easier for her to handle the situation this way.

As he watched her settle in one of the rear seats, rage rose in him, choking him, demanding he put his fist through the nearest wall. He didn't want this to be easy for her. He resented being relegated to the past with such controlled efficiency.

Drawing in a deep breath, he overruled the violent emotion raging through him, He had always managed to control it, but lately, more and more often, he had begun to wonder how much longer he could keep his control.

From her seat behind Garrick, Elise carefully avoided looking out the small window beside her. She took deep breaths and went through the multiplication table, trying to keep her mind off the distance between her body and solid ground. Mostly it didn't work. She had a handkerchief in her pocket to wipe away the perspiration that seemed to have permanently settled on the palms of her hands.

The first minutes of the flight had been filled

with polite talk among the four of them, then Charis, in the front passenger seat, began to steer the conversation into areas that excluded the two in the back, leaning toward Garrick as she talked. And as she talked, Max silently mimicked her expressions and gestures.

"Stop it," Elise whispered, her voice stern. "Stop making fun of her."

"Hey, I admire the lady. I can even see why old Gary's attracted to her," he whispered back. "She hangs on to every word that comes out of his mouth, like she's listening to the Burning Bush or something. And notice the way she always defers to his better judgment. Ego-building stuff. You have to admit, there's quite a contrast between you and Miss Submissive up there."

"Are you implying that living with me in some way emasculated Garrick? Just because I get a little stubborn about my independence some-times—"

Max gave a loud snort. "A little?" he asked. "A little stubborn? Hey, Garrick, we need an opinion back here. Ellie has just been generous enough to concede that she might be a little bullheaded about her independence. Would you say that's an objective observation?"

Garrick didn't respond immediately, and when he did, he didn't look back. "If Elise were any more autonomous," he said slowly, "they'd declare her an independent nation. 'Welcome to Brightland. Feel free to visit, but don't even think about trying to immigrate.'"

Frowning, she stared at the back of her husband's head. He was certainly in a strange mood today. "What kind of remark was that? Why would you say something like that?"

Before Garrick could answer, Charis turned in her seat and smiled at Elise. "Don't let these men get to you. I admire independent women. I really do. I wish I could be like you, but I can't seem to get the hang of being all on my own. I have a tremendous need for . . ."

"For the spotlight," Max muttered under his breath.

". . . a strong partner," Charis continued. "Someone I can depend on totally. Just the idea of being alone terrifies me. I don't think I could take it. I really don't. And, honestly, I believe there are some things only a man can handle." She gave a soft laugh. "I'm sure my attitude is frustrating for women's libbers and for sensible . . . um . . . robust types like you, Elise, but I can't help it. I guess I'll always be an old-fashioned girl at heart."

Leaning close to Elise, Max whispered, "I think I'm gonna puke."

Although it was obvious Charis hadn't heard Max, his movement toward Elise attracted her attention, and she took a moment to look him over thoroughly, not in a flirtatious way, but as though she was genuinely curious. Eventually her gaze settled on his face.

"Where did you meet Elise?" she asked finally.

Max cut his eyes toward Elise and grinned. "Somehow I get the impression Mrs. Hayden doesn't think I'm the proper kind of friend for a genteel little thing like you."

"She may have a point," Elise said. "I can't recall you ever making a push to be the proper kind of anything."

"Elise and Max have been friends since they were children," said Garrick, finally joining the conversation.

"We met in reform school," said Max, his expression sweetly innocent. When Elise sputtered with startled laughter, he added, "What's the matter, sugar, haven't you told anyone about your record?"

"Tell them you're teasing, Max," said Elise, her tone that of a patient mother.

Charis smiled at Garrick, a conspirator's smile. "We knew it, didn't we? Considering Garrick's position, he would never marry— What I mean is, he can't be associated with—"

"Scum?" Max suggested.

"Riffraff? Trash?" Elise offered helpfully.

"Lesser beings," was Garrick's dry contribution.

"That's it!" said Elise, laughing. "It confirms Mona's opinion of you anyway. She told me a couple of weeks ago you're nothing less than a saint."

"I've always liked your mother," said Garrick, giving his head a rueful shake, "but there are times I think she should have come with a label marked 'Batteries Not Included.'"

Throughout their teasing interchange Charis had glanced from one to the other of them, her expression bewildered. When she saw Elise watching her, she shrugged and changed the subject, giving an extended account of the fund-raiser in which she was currently involved.

Elise didn't listen for long. Her mind began to drift, and as she stared at the back of Garrick's head, she told herself it wasn't the lingering possessiveness she had acknowledged earlier making her believe Charis was wrong for him. It was nothing more than an objective opinion. A man like Garrick should be partnered by someone less self-centered, someone who shared his interests, someone more aware of the rest of the world.

Oh, wonderful, she thought with a rueful smile. Now she was trying to choose her husband's mistress for him. She had finally done the impossible. She had finally managed to outcivilize Garrick!

She had been quick enough to jump all over Max for minding Garrick's business. Now, she found herself doing the exact same thing. Maybe she wasn't quite as distant from her life as she had hoped.

"Elise . . . Elise, have you heard a word I've said?" Charis asked.

"I'm sorry—" She broke off, studying her husband's tense shoulder muscles. "What's wrong, Garrick?"

After an almost imperceptible hesitation he said, "There was no mention of that cloud in the weather report."

Leaning forward, Max looked through the

front windows. "Judas priest, where in hell did that come from? Can we go around it?"

Garrick gave his head a slight, frustrated shake. "I don't know. We might run into something worse. I think I'd better try to get above it." He began to ease the nose of the Cessna up.

Elise's heart seemed to move in several hard jerks, but before she had time to build up a good case of panic, they were already in the middle of a dark blue raging hell. The plane, growing mysteriously smaller, pitched and rolled like a fear-crazed animal as Garrick tried to force it through and above the unexpected storm system.

The driving rain seemed to Elise to entomb them in the plane, to seal them off from the rest of the world, magnifying and making more immediate every flash of lightning, every resounding clap of thunder.

After an interminably rough quarter hour their flight seemed to get smoother. Then, just as Elise was drawing in air to heave a sigh of relief, a million flashbulbs went off outside her window, and the Cessna was thrown violently away from the explosion, like a feather caught in a giant's sneeze.

"Holy hell," Elise whispered, the words inaudible over the sounds of Charis's panicky questions.

"What happened? What was that?" Diving toward Garrick, Charis clutched at his arm. "What exploded? Why is the plane doing that? *For God's sake, do something, Garrick!*"

Grasping Charis by the shoulders, Max hauled her out of her seat, switching places with her so he could sit next to Garrick.

Elise leaned forward in her seat, straining to hear their conversation over the blond's hysterical babbling.

"Char— Charis. *Charis!*" She grabbed the other woman's arm to get her attention. "Will you please stop predicting my death? There are no terrorists, and that wasn't a bomb. We were hit by lightning, but we're not going to die. Do you hear me? Charis—"

Nothing Elise said seemed to penetrate the woman's terror. Finally, in desperation, Elise slapped her hard on one smooth cheek. The screams stopped abruptly, and Charis covered her face with her hands, sobbing quietly.

"Try to control yourself," Elise said firmly. "Hysterics won't help. You should be—"

She broke off and bit her lip. What was she doing? Even if Garrick somehow managed to control the damaged plane, there was no place to land it. They were flying over southeastern Oklahoma with nothing below them except miles and miles of treecovered hills.

The plane was going down, and Charis was probably right. It was very likely they were all going to die. If the other woman wanted to end her life on a hysterical note, Elise had no right to stop her.

Leaning back in her seat, Elise squeezed her eyes closed and began to pray. She didn't ask God to keep the plane in the air. She had lived long enough to know He didn't work that way. Instead, she prayed for the strength to face what was ahead. She prayed for courage. She prayed her last minutes of life wouldn't be wasted on fear.

She tried to concentrate completely on the prayer, but the bucking motion of the plane kept intruding on her thoughts. She was too aware of the Cessna's continued descent, too aware of the man in the pilot seat, fighting for control of the plane, fighting a battle that was impossible to win.

Her gaze was riveted on the back of her husband's neck. She memorized the straining tendons, assigning what little strength she possessed to him as her mind was flooded with dark and vague images, dark and vague regrets. Too late. Too late to pull it all together. Too late to find the one who was waiting to love her. Too late.

Leaning her head against the seat back, she gripped the armrests with urgent fingers as she felt the Cessna lurch to the side with a rough, shuddering movement.

This is it, Elise told herself. This is it.

She heard someone call out her name just moments before the plane collided with the earth.

Five

Elise wasn't sure whether she lost consciousness or simply checked out of reality for a while. She knew only that her return to awareness was accompanied by the sound of a woman screaming. There seemed no end to the ear-piercing screams, no pauses or hesitations. Why, she asked herself, didn't the woman run out of breath the way any ordinary human being would?

She believed she heard other voices, believed she heard her name being called again and again. But were the voices real . . . or creations of her imagination? The darkness, all-encompassing, added to her disorientation. Her mind skittered over ideas, heaved to and fro with thoughts—black holes in space . . . Poe's House of Usher . . . a black-and-white forties movie version of a lunatic asylum.

"The Snake Pit?" she murmured.

She couldn't see where she was, and she couldn't see the woman whose continual screeching chafed her nerves.

"Ellie?"

When the voice finally reached her through the screams, Elise frowned. It was strange, but the voice sounded like . . .

"Max?" she whispered.

She felt so confused. What was Max doing in her snake pit? She knew her brain wasn't functioning all that well, but she could have sworn Max was across the world, living as a recluse deep in a Japanese jungle.

"Ellie! You've got to get out of here. And for God's sake, take her with you. Come on, little star, move your butt!"

"I can't see. Why is it so dark, Max? Why—" Abruptly, inevitably, she remembered everything. She remembered the dark cloud that appeared from nowhere. She remembered the storm and the lightning. She remembered Garrick fighting for control of the—

"Where's Garrick!" The words erupted from her, her voice hoarse with fear. She struggled against the restricting safety belt. "Max, can you see him? Garrick!"

"I'm here, Elise."

Garrick's voice, coming from somewhere above her, was as composed as always. An enormous wave of relief washed over her, weakening her, and after a moment she gave a short, helpless laugh. God bless him, he never changed. So calm. So collected. So civilized.

"It's dark because we landed in heavy foliage," Garrick continued in a soft, soothing tone. "I want you to get out as quickly as you can, Elise. We may have a fuel leak."

She marveled that Garrick could use his normal, coolly modulated voice to inform her the plane might very well blow up at any second.

Drawing in a sharp breath, Elise released her safety belt and pulled herself up out of the seat. Movement was awkward—the plane seemed to have landed at a steep angle—and after falling back into her seat twice, she more or less threw herself sideways toward the sound of what she now recognized as Charis's screams. When she reached the other woman, Elise brailled her way up the rounded shoulders, found Charis's face, and as she had in a time that seemed so long ago, she slapped her.

"That's better," she and Max said simultaneously when the high-pitched screeching abruptly stopped.

"Can she walk?" Max asked. "It takes both of us to hold the door open . . . tree limbs against it . . . I've got a bum leg and Garrick hurt his hand, but if you need help—"

"We're fine," Elise said through clenched teeth as she pulled Charis out of her seat.

Dragging the blond along with her, Elise grasped the front passenger seat to pull the two of them up toward the door. Caught in an anxiety-induced time warp, hours, days, an entire lifetime, passed before she finally managed to shove Charis ahead of her and out the door.

Even then, even when Elise was outside the plane and could at last see her hand in front of her face, it wasn't over. It took the combined efforts of the three functioning survivors to get Charis across branches and the scratchy growth of the cedar trees, and, finally, to lower her to the ground.

When Garrick and Max dropped down beside Elise and Charis, the two men, as though they shared a single mind, each took one of the blond's arms and half dragged, half carried her away from the plane.

For a long time, as they stood in a narrow clearing and waited, no one spoke. Each expected at any second to hear the explosion, to see the burst of flames that would destroy what was left of the Cessna. But after about half an hour of waiting, Elise finally allowed herself to believe it wasn't going to happen. The danger of explosion and fire had passed.

That was when words began to flow from them in erratic, disjointed bits of conversation.

"Has anyone seen my other shoe?"

"Hold still, you have growing things caught in your hair."

"Did I ever tell you I'm allergic to cedar?"

"For heaven's sake, I feel like Peg-leg Pete."

Then, in what seemed like an orchestrated reaction, Garrick, Elise, and Max began to laugh. It was a release of tension, a ceremony held to honor life. Charis simply sat on the ground, too limp, too dazed, to join them or to resent them.

Incredibly, the clearing where they stood was dry. Only a short while earlier they had been caught up in a granddaddy thunderstorm. Elise could see flashes to the east and occasionally heard the low rumble of distant thunder. But where they stood, the ground was dry, and a watered-down version of the sun was visible low on the western horizon.

"You're a mess," she scolded Max as she tied a handkerchief around the swelling bruise on his calf. "Streaks of green and brown and red all over your face, you look like a Sherwin Williams sample board."

He thumped her arm. "How about showing a little respect for a wounded hero?"

"You were terrific," she said as she glanced over to where Garrick sat leaning against a tree with Charis huddled close beside him. She didn't like the way he held his scarred hand cradled against his chest, but when she had asked him to let her look at it, he had stiffly told her it was fine.

Wounded hero? Stubborn fool.

Following her gaze, Max said, "That day we met in your office, I didn't like him. I'm not sure I do now, but I have to admit he's really something. Do you realize that if anyone else had been piloting the plane, we'd all be dead now? Look at this clearing. It's not much wider than a country road." He shook his head, his eyes reflecting awe and incredulity. "I think he must have willed the son of a gun to go where he wanted it to."

In a louder voice, one meant to carry, Max said, "I have to hand it to you, Garrick. You really know how to keep your guests entertained. What have you got planned for tomorrow—flood, earthquake, a peasant uprising?"

A smile twitched Garrick's strong lips as he rose to his feet, leaving Charis curled up on the ground, still crying—but softly now. "Actually, it could be worse," he said as he joined them.

"We could be dead," said Elise, her voice wry. "Dead would probably be worse."

Garrick's smile was more pronounced this time. "That's number one on the plus side. We're all alive. The plane came down in a firebreak, so the tail can be seen by anyone searching for us."

"Number two," Max said.

"Number three is food," Garrick continued. "I know the stuff I brought in the cooler isn't exactly exciting, but it'll help us keep going."

"How long before they start looking for us?" asked Elise, trying for a tone that was even and unconcerned.

Garrick spent the next few minutes explaining how rescue operations worked, but he very carefully managed to avoid answering her question.

"And the minus side?" Max asked when Garrick had finished. "Have you got a list for the minuses? I don't mean the obvious ones, like the plane coming down in the hills of Oklahoma instead of someplace interesting. I mean the drawbacks we haven't thought of yet."

"Just one," Garrick said. "We don't know how far we veered off the flight plan before we came down."

His quietly spoken words were followed by somber silence. Elise knew that before the storm knocked out the radio, Garrick had tried to maintain contact with the ground, but there had been too much interference for any kind of communication.

"Someone may have seen us come down," Max said finally. "You never know, we could be picked up first thing in the morning."

"*Morning!*"

The screeched word took them by surprise, and they all swung around. Charis had come suddenly to life. Rising shakily to her feet, she walked toward them. The pink suit was a sad-looking thing, and she had lost her hat. Dirt and tears had left vivid streaks on her face, and her blond hair stood away from her face in unkempt wisps. In the fading light she looked wild. She looked like a madwoman.

"What are you talking about? You're only saying these things to torment me. We're going to be rescued tonight. Do you hear me? We have to be rescued *tonight*! I can't sleep out here." Her voice began to rise in pitch, velocity, and volume. "Damn you all to hell. You act as though we're on a backyard camp-out. The plane crashed. The freaking plane *crashed*! I've got to get out of here. Get me out of here, dammit! You've got—"

As her words dwindled into frantic incoherence, the blond's voice continued to rise, and when she looked in danger of having a self-induced stroke, Elise sighed and shot a glance toward the men. Garrick kept his frowning gaze on Charis, but he didn't move.

"You want to handle it this time?" Elise asked Max.

He shrugged, and without warning reached out to slap Charis sharply across the cheek. The blond's eyes opened wide in shock. Seconds later she slumped to the ground and covered her face with her hands.

"I'm going to check out the plane," Garrick said abruptly. "Max?"

"Right behind you, Kemo Sabe," said Max, allowing Elise to help him to his feet.

Elise watched them go then sat down on a large, smooth rock, her elbows on her knees, her chin resting in the palms of her hands as she listened to the sounds of silence. She should have gone with the men. Charis, poor soul, was too much out of it to offer a distraction, and Elise felt a little guilty for not being able to share the blond's desperation.

The truth was, selfish or not, Elise needed a distraction. She didn't want to think about the minutes before and after the crash.

But of course she couldn't think about anything else. She thought about everything—the terror before, when she believed they were all going to die; and the terror afterward, when she thought something had happened to Garrick.

In a moment of reluctant revelation she admitted something important to herself: The separation hadn't completely severed those proverbial ties that bind. Love had existed between them. Nothing could change that, not even divorce. She had given a part of herself to Garrick, and wherever he went, whatever he did, he would carry part of her with him always.

Rising restlessly to her feet, she glanced over her shoulder at Charis. "You want to help me gather some wood for a fire? It would give us something to do."

She might as well have tried to hold a conversation with the trees. Charis was in her own world, and judging by the way her shoulders shook, it wasn't a pleasant place.

"That's all right," Elise told her, as if the blond had spoken. "You stay here and rest. I'll just go a little way into the trees to look for fallen branches. If you need me, just yell."

She hadn't taken more than two steps into the woods when Charis let out a bloodcurdling scream.

Swinging around, Elise ran to her side. "What is it? What happened?"

"I can't—You can't leave me here alone."

Elise pushed the hair off her forehead and counted to ten. "There's no wood out here in the clearing," she explained patiently. "I promise I won't go far."

Before Elise had even finished her sentence,

Charis began shaking her head back and forth in a vehement denial. "No . . . no, no!"

Exhaling through her teeth, Elise said, "You have two choices. You can stay here and wait for the men, or you can come with me."

Seconds later she entered the woods again. This time Charis was beside her, hugging Elise's arm tightly to her breasts, crowding every step she took.

Elise felt a bit like Dorothy, entering the dark woods of Oz with a trembling, moaning Scarecrow clinging fervently to her side. *Lions and tigers and bears, oh my. Lions and tigers and bears, oh my.*

"You don't mind my holding on to you, do you?" Charis whispered.

"It makes walking a tiny bit difficult, but I'll try to look on the positive side."

"There's a positive side?"

"Sure. If we run into any lonely backwoods types, they'll probably think we're gay and leave us alone. Charis . . . Charis, for heaven's sake, I was just teasing. Stop moaning. And don't you dare faint."

Charis stopped moaning, and she didn't faint, but every time Elise bent down to pick up a piece of dead wood, Charis, still clutching her arm, would bend right along with her.

"What was that?" Charis whispered when they had been in the woods for several minutes.

"What? I didn't hear anything."

"It was a kind of swishing noise. Back there in those bushes."

Elise stood still and listened. Sure enough, after a moment she heard small rustling sounds in the dead leaves.

"Swishing is okay," she said, her voice soothing. "Swishing and rustling mean small. Crashing, now that would be a different thing altogether. Crashing, banging, or pounding would mean 'run like hell.'"

"Oh God, oh God, oh God."

"I was teasing again. Look, if you really want to be my friend, you'll loosen up. And while you're at it, how about loosening your grip on my arm. You're cutting off the circulation. Here, carry some of the wood."

Due to some obscure anatomical defect, the blond wasn't capable of handling more than three small branches without dropping them, but by the time Garrick and Max returned from the plane, Elise had managed to get a respectable campfire going in the clearing.

The men had brought the cooler with them, and although Max proposed counting the cheese doodles to discourage pilfering, no one showed an interest in food. The events of the day had taken a toll on them, and as darkness fell, the conversation began to dwindle.

Garrick shifted his position, being careful of the hand throbbing painfully with every movement. Beside him, Charis was whispering an unending complaint, but he didn't catch more than one word in ten. All his concentration was centered on the woman across the campfire, watching her laugh and enjoy herself with her good friend Max.

It was almost funny, he told himself. They had just barely survived a plane crash, but all his thoughts were taken up by a woman who no longer wanted him.

Why did she have to be so damn brave, so damn together? Was there no virtue the gods hadn't given to her? Brains, beauty, and a courageous heart. All the attributes to set her above ordinary women. All the attributes to make her irresistible to men.

Garrick's own private obsession had nothing to do with her looks, or even with her mind. Some intangible something bound him to her . . . with unbreakable ties. And at that moment, as he watched her captivating another man, Garrick wished with all his heart she were ugly and dull and had all the frailties of an ordinary woman. Then the appreciation of her would be his privilege alone.

"Garrick . . . Garrick, you have to take me back to the plane. My head is pounding so dreadfully, I can hardly think."

When Charis's voice broke into his introspection, Garrick turned to look at her and exhaled a slow breath. He should have been grateful for the distraction. He should have welcomed the chance to get away from Elise and her good friend Max.

But as he took Charis's arm and walked away from the fire, he couldn't help glancing back over his shoulder, meeting Decatur's innocently inquiring gaze with a look that was clearly a warning.

From her seat on a large gray rock, Elise watched the retreating pair until they disappeared, then turned back to find Max studying her features intently.

With a sound of irritated disbelief, he shook his head slowly from side to side. "You people are too much. Talk about strange cultures. Did I miss out on something, some revolution or divine edict, while I was out of the country? Last I remember, wives—even soon-to-be-ex-wives— didn't sit quietly by while their husbands walked off into the proverbial sunset with little blond bimbos."

Elise leaned toward the fire, holding her hands out to it. "Tell me some more about life on your Japanese island. When did you decide you had enough material for a book?"

Max, bless him, didn't quarrel with her change of subject. Without comment, he began to tell her about the ways of the people and about the terrain of the little island. It was one of hundreds of islands in the Ryukyu group and had captured his imagination. He explained how he had found himself becoming more and more fascinated by the ageless quality of the islanders' faces and by the ancient customs still being followed.

Eventually, however, he stopped talking and

rose awkwardly to his feet, favoring his injured leg. "I guess we'd better hit the sack. Pull the shade on a really fun day. No telling what tomorrow will—" He broke off and turned his head to meet her gaze. "Sooner or later, Ellie, we have to join them in the plane."

She wanted to argue with him. She wanted to say, *Like hell we do*. But she didn't think she could explain to Max why she was so reluctant to join Garrick and Charis. She couldn't explain to him because she wasn't sure she could explain it to herself.

Elise shouldn't have worried. Whatever she had suspected, whatever intimacy she had dreaded walking into, was absent when they reached the plane. Garrick and Charis were simply sitting in the forward seats talking quietly.

Although the Cessna had settled some, there was still a noticeable tilt to it, and it took almost an hour to remove the four rear seats in order to make room for them to stretch out to sleep.

"I've never slept standing up before," Elise said as she worked to spread her clothes, the only available bedding, on her portion of the cleared area.

"I have," Max said from somewhere nearby.

Those two words were the signal for giddiness. They were all exhausted, and it was a little like being drunk. The smallest thing triggered their laughter. Max's adventures in an Afghani mountain village, the tale of how he and his native guide had been forced to sleep on a narrow mountain ledge, brought spurts of helpless laughter from both Garrick and Elise. It was almost an hour before they settled down, conversation becoming sporadic.

Elise's eyelids were growing heavy when she felt someone moving close beside her. "Max?" she whispered.

"No," Garrick said curtly. "Not Max."

"Oh."

"We're still married, Elise." His voice was calm and quiet as he settled beside her. "And as long as we are, my place is beside you."

She almost argued with him. She almost reminded him of how many times he had not been at her side. Of how many times he had chosen to be beside Charis instead. What stopped her was amazement that she would even think of tackling the subject—now, after coming through the crash of their plane; now, at the end of their marriage. How ludicrous, she thought, to discuss his nearness or lack of it at a time like this.

"Did you have a pleasant tête-a-tête with your good friend Max?" he asked, his voice mocking.

"Pleasant," she affirmed. "And your talk with your date? Was it . . . enlightening?"

A soft laugh escaped him. "That's not exactly the word I would have chosen." After a moment's pause he said, "I promised I would get you safely to Springfield. I'm sorry, Elise."

"Don't be silly. I knew you would be blaming yourself, and it's so stupid," she murmured. "You've got a lot of strength, Garrick, but not even you can hold back a thunderstorm."

She paused, her thoughts thrown back to the crash. "It's funny how almost dying, how almost leaving life behind, makes you appreciate it more. I have never felt quite so alive as I did when the four of us ran away from the plane. I felt I could run forever. There was fear, but I honestly think the feeling of exhilaration was stronger. It was as though I had fought a battle and won. I wanted to laugh or do a cartwheel, something really silly to thumb my nose at death."

"I think we all felt the same way." The low, husky quality of Garrick's voice was hypnotically soothing. "Falling out of the sky is fairly effective at reminding you you're mortal. Then, when you walk away from a crash like this, when you realize all the odds were against you walking away, you feel almost superhuman. We were attacked by a force a million times more powerful than our combined strength, and we survived. We beat it. Pretty heady stuff."

As she listened to the quietly spoken words, Elise was reminded of how often in their two years of marriage they had had similar conversations. There had always been something to talk about, something to debate. And yet she was speaking the truth when she had told Max that the number-one reason for their breakup had been the lack of communication. Because talking wasn't always communication.

She and Garrick had been merely two articulate, intelligent people objectively discussing subjects, and it seemed to Elise that people involved in a personal relationship should manage occasionally to be subjective. They should be able to throw some heart into a conversation as well as brain.

Talking to Garrick, hearing his views on politics, religion, or a movie they had just attended, had given her some insights into his personality, but it was like watching the steam coming from a heated pool; the rising mist was an indication of the warmth of the pool, but only touch gave a measure of that warmth, the depth of it. She had never been allowed to test for Garrick's depths. She had never been allowed close to the essence of the man.

"Too late," she murmured, her drowsiness showing in her slurred speech. After a moment she laughed softly.

"What?" he whispered in the darkness. "What's funny?"

"Have you ever noticed the way your thoughts take on a life of their own when you're falling asleep? I started thinking about what we were going to do tomorrow, then suddenly I was picturing Clark Kent undressing in a telephone booth. And I can't figure out how I got there. The thought had to start somewhere. How do you get from watching for search planes to playing voyeur with Superman?"

"Maybe it's your mind's way of preparing you for what's coming," he offered, his dark voice distracted, as though he were thinking of something other than their conversation.

"What do you mean?" she prompted.

"What's going to happen if we're not picked up tomorrow? I have a feeling Decatur can hold his own in any environment, but for you and me, for Charis . . . There are going to be changes, Elise. The disguises are going to come off, and for better or for worse, we won't be the same people we were back in the city."

The disguises were all going to come off.

Although he was probably right, Elise wasn't sure she liked what he was saying. She had seen glimpses of the changes. And she didn't know if she could handle what might come next.

Six

Elise awakened to morning light and something moving beneath her . . . that something in fact might have been what brought her awake.

Slowly opening her eyes, she discovered her body was pressed between the metal wall of the plane and Garrick, whom she seemed to be overlapping.

Glancing up, she saw he was watching her, his dark eyes trained intently on her face.

"Gravity," he explained, his voice rough with the remnants of sleep.

She nodded slowly, understanding that overnight Newton had pushed them into this tangled heap.

"What? Why do you stare like that?" he asked. When she didn't answer, he rubbed his chin with his right hand. "I suppose I need a shave."

After a moment she said, "You hate that, don't

you? You can't stand the fact that there are six or seven hours out of every twenty-four when you're not in complete control. Your beard grows without your permission. Your mind, in dreams, takes off in unauthorized directions." Her voice was low and husky as she taunted him. "I always liked you best early in the morning before you slipped into the pinstriped, spit-and-polish perfection. In the early morning you're not quite so civilized. You don't have enough brain cells working to worry about society's rules. In the early morning, only your senses are working at full strength."

When the banked force that was habitually in his eyes flared, she experienced a moment of triumph. But only a moment. With startlingly abrupt movements he shifted, reversing their positions so that he held her body pinned beneath his. Grasping her chin with his right hand, he rubbed his thumb across her bottom lip with rough strokes.

"Are you sure you know what you're doing?" he asked, and now his voice was husky with something other than sleep.

She wanted to say, *Not a plain no, but hell no.* She had no idea what she was doing. Some instinct she didn't understand had prompted her to speak. She only knew that she was suddenly, unexpectedly afraid.

As though he recognized the uncertainty in her, his fingers tightened on her chin, and he gave a rough laugh. "Too late, Elise."

His mouth closed over hers before he had

finished speaking. Taken off guard, she struggled, pressing her lips tightly together in a last-ditch attempt at sanity, but when he nipped at her lower lip, a surge of familiar, white-hot desire shot through her, taking control of her body away from her, parting her lips, sinking her fingers into the bare flesh of his shoulders.

She had expected anger, an outward show of what she had seen in his eyes, and she could have handled it. She was prepared for it. But this was hunger, so blatant, so powerful, she had no defenses against it. And she had no way of keeping her own hunger from rising to match it.

"Will you kindly get your foot out of my face?"

A long moment passed before Elise recognized the voice. Charis's voice. Pulling away from Garrick, Elise reluctantly met his eyes. Night-dark eyes. Eyes that could see forever. Eyes that had once held eternity.

Shivering with a combination of self-blame and leftover desire, she glanced away from him. Charis was pulling herself into a sitting position as she grumbled unintelligible complaints about the night just past.

"Our little princess is not a happy camper," Max said from his position on the other side of the blond. "I think she found a nasty old pea under her mattress."

"That was the most unbearably uncomfortable night I've ever spent in my life," Charis moaned. "I didn't sleep for a single minute." She turned her gaze on Max. "You kicked me. Why on earth would you want to kick me?"

"I wasn't kicking you. I was just trying to move you over. I don't know why you're complaining. Try sleeping with an elbow in the kidney sometime. And if I get gangrene in my leg, we'll all know who to blame. Every time you moved, you managed to land on top of it."

"Children, children," Elise scolded. "Put on your happy faces or there'll be no dessert for you tonight."

She ducked when one of Max's shoes came sailing toward her, barely missing her head. Laughing, she tried several times to get to her feet, but kept falling back against Garrick. It was only when he lent her a hand, his good hand, that she finally managed to work free of the cover and crawl on all fours toward the pile of luggage.

After finding her valise, she climbed the rest of the way to the door. "If anyone needs me, I'll be in my dressing room," she said as she hoisted herself out of the plane.

Stooping beside the campfire, Garrick poked at the slow blaze, urging it on. He had been there a while when Max, coming from the direction of the plane, hobbled toward the fire with the aid of a crutch he had fashioned from a limb.

Elise's friend was a strange man. He seemed to take being stranded in the wilderness in stride, as though it happened to him every day or so. Maybe that was yet another source of the feeling of hostility Garrick felt toward him.

Or maybe not, Garrick told himself wryly as he

thought of the warmth that existed in Elise's relationship with Max. The warmth and ease. With her good friend Max, she was approachable. With Max, she became a woman Garrick had never been allowed to know.

He was still frowning when Elise walked into the clearing. She had changed into loose-fitting brown slacks and an oversized brown and rust shirt made of a gauzy material, the sleeves rolled up to midforearm. The shirt had slipped off one smooth shoulder, but on Elise it looked as though that was exactly how the designer had planned it. How could she look as elegant and sophisticated, here in the wilderness, as she did at a society ball?

Last night, Garrick had told her they would all change, but he saw no change in her. She was still a closely guarded work of art. It was Garrick himself who had changed. Something was growing inside him, an overpowering determination not just to have her, but to reach her. To really reach her.

And then, no matter what happened in the future, Elise would not be able to dismiss his memory lightly. He would make sure of it.

As he continued stirring the fire, listening with half an ear to the sounds of Max and Charis's bickering, Garrick began to make his plans.

Elise glanced up in surprise when Charis knocked Max's crutch out from under him and stalked away.

"You really need to work on your people skills," Elise told him.

"She's out of cigarettes," Max explained as he struggled to his feet, "and she's feeling a little testy."

"If you learned that, why did you keep picking at her?"

He shrugged. "You know me, danger is my business."

"You're brain-dead." She stood up and dusted off her slacks. "I'm going to find the water I smelled last night."

"You smelled it?" said Max, drawing back his head to stare at her. "You can really smell it? I could get a fortune for you in the desert."

"At dusk, when the air gets heavy, the smells are stronger," she said, "and I kept catching the musty, decaying odor of plants growing in and around— Why am I explaining this to you? You're a very irritating person, Max."

"I do my best."

Garrick hadn't said a word, but when Elise began to move away, he rose to his feet, frowning as he shoved his left hand into the pocket of his chinos. "I don't like the idea of you wandering around alone."

"I'll leave a trail of bread crumbs," she said, keeping her voice light. "I'm not a reckless person, Garrick. I won't take a chance on getting lost."

The last words were thrown casually over her shoulder as she walked away, but Elise didn't feel casual. In fact, it took all the control she could muster to keep from running.

As soon as she had put a sufficient amount of woods between herself and the others, she kicked out viciously at a flowering shrub, misguidedly trying to release some of her tension.

She had no one to blame for these new feelings of tension, no one but herself. Of her own free will she had goaded Garrick into losing control. She had done it intentionally—and she knew it. But she didn't understand the reason behind such an unreasonable, not to mention dangerous, course of action. What on earth had she hoped to gain by such childish, irrational behavior?

Leaning against a tree, she thought back to the night two weeks earlier when Garrick had come to the house. Before he had joined her, she had immersed herself in the past, tracing their steps leading to the present. And it had seemed to her the breakup of her marriage had been too controlled, too neat. She had recognized in herself melancholy and regret. What she hadn't recognized, until this moment, was the blow her ego had taken. And it had definitely taken a blow.

Pride was the culprit, she told herself in disgust. Her stupid pride had dictated her actions, whispering devious thoughts in her ears until she had acted the fool. She had taunted Garrick, mocking him intentionally because, selfishly, she wanted to leave some kind of mark on him. She wanted to put a dent, if only a small one, in his cast-iron facade. Something that would say, "Elise was here."

It was a small-minded, ignoble thing to have done, not like her at all. Which only proved Garrick was right. The crash and the isolation were already changing her. And not for the better.

She pushed away from the tree and began moving through the woods, resenting Garrick for being the cause of her downfall, resenting herself for not having a stronger will.

It's not that bad, she told herself after a while. *I'm young and I'm intelligent. So what if I've discovered I've got a little-bitty mean streak? It could be a lot worse. I could be old and stupid and mean.*

The excuse she had used to get away from the others, telling them she was going to search for water, had been nothing more than a fabrication that had popped into her mind. So, seconds later, when she'd pushed through some chest-high bushes and almost fallen into a small stream, she had been completely off guard.

"What do you know?" she murmured in surprise. "There really was water."

The stream had cut into the land, leaving steep banks on either side, and the water, looking cool and clear, was no more than a foot deep as it ran swiftly over rocks that glistened in the sun.

Slipping out of her sandals, she rolled up the legs of her slacks and more or less slid down the six-foot bank to reach the stream. Her first tentative step into the water brought a shocked squeak from her, and she shivered as the icy-cold liquid swirled around her ankles. She stood still until her flesh adjusted to the lowered temperature before wading out to the middle where a large, square boulder thrust its shoulders out of the shallow water.

Resting on the sun-warmed rock, she dangled her feet in the water and concentrated on becoming part of the boulder. Of course she was disregarding the passing minutes. Of course she was counting on her rock . . . for it knew nothing of time.

Surprisingly she almost succeeded in reaching Nirvana. Minutes ceased to tick abruptly away. They eased smoothly around her, ignoring her as easily as she ignored them.

She had no idea how long she had been sitting in the sun when she heard a voice coming from somewhere to her right.

"So you found it after all."

Swinging her head toward the bank, she saw Garrick standing with his hands shoved in his pockets, leaning one shoulder against a small oak.

"I just followed my nose," she said, then glancing at her watch, she grimaced an apology. "I didn't realize I had been here so long." Pushing off the rock, she waded toward him. When she reached the side, he knelt and leaned down to help her climb the bank.

"What are the others doing?" she asked as

they turned and she followed him back through the heavy foliage.

"They were still arguing when I left."

She glanced at him. "I'm not sure you should have left Charis alone with Max."

"A week ago I might have worried about her," he said, his firm lips twisting in a small, wry smile. "Not now. I've recently come to realize that Charis's greatest strength is her vulnerability."

"Maybe. Maybe that would work if she were dealing with any ordinary man, but I wouldn't count on those misty blue eyes to save her from Max. He's a good friend, but he can be cruel. Especially to women like Charis. Soft women. Women who count on their femininity to smooth away any problem that confronts them." She paused, biting her lip. "That sounded rather bitchy, didn't it?"

He shrugged. "You didn't say anything that Charis wouldn't confirm—in different words, of course. She makes no bones about—"

He broke off abruptly, flinching as a low-hanging branch slapped against his left hand.

"Is your hand still painful?"

His lips tightened. "It's all right."

"Yes, that's what you said last night. If it's all right, why did you wince when that limb brushed against it? Let me look at it and see for myself it's okay. Then I'll stop nagging you."

"You never nag."

"Sure I do. I've just learned how to do it artfully. Sneaky nagging."

"You mean you pretend," he said, his voice

suddenly harsh. "You don't have to tell me about it. After more than two years of polite pretense, I'm an expert on the subject."

She stared at him, her brow creasing in bewilderment at the cynicism in his tone. In a moment she realized he had intentionally insulted her. He wanted to make her angry enough to divert her attention from his hand.

How many times in the past had she passively accepted a change of subject? How many times had she suppressed her need to know because she didn't want to annoy him?

Their marriage was over. There was no longer any need for her to tiptoe around him. She didn't have to pretend to be tolerant. She didn't have to pretend to be detached. If it had accomplished nothing else, the disintegration of her marriage had set her free. She could be a world-class bitch if she wanted. She could be herself.

"You want the gloves off?" she asked slowly. "That suits me fine. Just who in hell do you think you are?" Her features tightened with rage. "Or, more to the point, who in hell do you think I am? I'll tell you who I'm *not*. I'm not a stranger you pass on the street. And I'm not one of your employees. We were married for two years. Two blasted years! I'm entitled to something from you, even if it's only a little leftover intimacy. Stop acting like an idiot, and let me see your damned hand! Now, Garrick."

He did as he was told, but his narrow-eyed, watchful expression forced a dry laugh from her. "You don't have to look so— For heaven's sake,

Garrick," she exclaimed. "This is a deep cut." Her tone softened as she examined his hand. "Why on earth are you being so stubborn about it?" She looked around. "I need to clean it so I can get a better look at it. I think there was a place downstream from here where we could get to the water without having to rappel down the bank."

He didn't argue as they walked back to the stream or even when she made him sit on a rock while she wet his handkerchief in the stream. He simply watched her, steadily, silently, as though he were trying to figure out what kind of game she was playing.

"I've got some astringent in my makeup case," she said, kneeling beside him to clean the cut. "I'll put it on when we get back." She glanced up at him. "It'll probably sting like hell, but it will kill off some of the germs you've been breeding here. Besides, you deserve the pain for being so damned pigheaded."

Still he didn't say a word, and neither did he take his eyes off her.

She exhaled slowly. "Look, I know. . . . I can understand why you're sensitive about the scars on your hand, but you can't be stupid." She smiled up at him. "You're Garrett Hewitt Fane. You're not allowed to be stupid. All those old dead New Hampshire Fanes would hunt you up and rattle their platinum chains while they explain the family code. You can be unscrupulous. You can be mean and nasty and downright ruthless. They'd probably even let you evict a few old ladies from property you own, but Fanes must never, never make asses of themselves."

"I've never evicted any old ladies."

She laughed. "You know what I mean." She paused, unable to meet his eyes as she continued, "Isn't it about time you forgot about how this"—she nodded toward the hand she held between both of hers—"looks? No one notices. They notice that you hide it, but if you ignored it, so would they. I promise you, a scarred hand isn't what people remember after meeting you for the first time."

In his eyes the unnamed emotion flared again. It startled her, and she almost pulled back. She had to tell herself again that she was through backing down. She was through living a polite, civilized lie.

"So you don't want me to talk about it," she said. "Well, that's tough. You said we would all change. I don't know about the others, but I'm changing. I'm changing back to me. I refuse to play the gutless wonder ever again. I don't have to pretend to be your sort of perfect, sophisticated woman anymore. The reasons for that charade no longer exist. But there are still things I want to know. Things I wanted to ask during our marriage but didn't for fear of offending."

"Such as?" he asked stiffly.

"Such as, what happened to your hand?"

"It was burned."

She sighed heavily. "That's obvious. How did it get burned? What happened?"

"What do you want from me?" His voice had lost its stiffness and was just plain angry. "Why are you doing this?"

"Vulgar curiosity?" she offered tightly, her anger rising to meet his.

He drew in a slow, deep breath and shook his head in denial. "No, not just curiosity. I know you better. Okay, why not? I burned my hand when my sister's house caught on fire."

"You were inside when it caught on fire?"

"No, I got there later."

Her throat tightened painfully. "You went into a burning house?" she whispered.

"There wasn't anyone else. No one but me." He gave his head a sharp shake. "Not that I did any good. I was too late. Paula didn't make it."

"I'm sorry, Garrick," she said slowly.

She had known his sister was dead, but it was all she knew. It must have been hell for him. For a man like Garrick, a man whose force of will was so exceptionally strong, failing to save his sister must have come close to destroying him. She knew the scars on his hand were insignificant compared to what the failure to save his sister must have done to him emotionally.

"I've never met anyone as shy as Paula," he said quietly. "She was three years older, but you would never have known it. There was a naive quality about her, a fairy-tale innocence she kept even as an adult." He paused. "My parents never understood that part of her. Perhaps I didn't either, but I didn't have to understand her to love her. They never loved— No, that's not fair.

They loved her, but they didn't like her very much. They were ashamed of her. Strangers confused Paula. New situations overwhelmed her. She couldn't participate in their world, and they made her life miserable because of what they saw as a deficiency in her."

Elise stared at him in open wonder. This was the first direct, unsolicited information Garrick had ever given her about either his sister or his parents. She knew his mother had died six years earlier of a stroke, and his father lived abroad, somewhere on the French Riviera. They had received a stiffly worded telegram from Mr. Fane congratulating them on their marriage, but as far as she knew, it was the only time Garrick had heard from him in the two years they had been married.

"When Paula turned twenty-five," he continued quietly, "she convinced Mother that she should have her own place, a small house they built for her on the grounds of our home in Manchester. She called it her little cabin in the woods. She said she could pretend to be independent there, pretend our parents weren't supporting her. She could pretend she had a real life.

"She did the decorating herself, and it was like a storybook cottage. Rose trellises all around it. Lots of white lace inside. I think she was happy there. She wrote poetry, free verse that she never let anyone see. No one but me. They were dark, violent poems. Sometimes I'm glad they were all destroyed in the fire."

There was a long silence, and Elise had begun to think he wouldn't continue when he started speaking again, slowly, quietly, as though he were talking to himself. "The fire started in the kitchen. While she was asleep. She died of smoke inhalation, you know. They told me it wasn't painful . . . she simply didn't wake up.

"I was home from college for spring break, and I had been busy with friends for several days, but I finally found time to visit my sister. I remember walking along the brick path leading to her cottage. It was twilight, clear and beautiful, with the smell of new growth and smoke in the air.

"Oh yes," he said as he noticed her startled movement, "I smelled the smoke. That's the really damnable part. The part that sticks in my mind most vividly. I smelled the smoke long before I got there, but it was a thing barely on the edge of my mind. When you smell smoke, you think, Someone's burning leaves. Or barbecuing. It doesn't occur to you a house could be on fire.

"In a movie, there's always music, building and building in the background, to warn the audience that something critical is about to happen. But there wasn't any music." His muscles contracted, leaving his features tight and hard. "Dammit, why don't they play the freaking music in real life? Something that tells you to hurry, to run like hell because something is about to happen."

His nostrils flared as he drew in a rough

breath. "The closer I got, the stronger the smell of smoke was, and it finally connected. I ran the rest of the way. When I got there, the flames hadn't spread to the bedroom, but the kitchen and most of the living room— When I opened the door to the bedroom, I let it in. *I let it in.* You wouldn't believe how fast a fire can spread. I felt like I was racing it. I-I can't picture what the room looked like, I guess I couldn't see for the smoke, but I managed to make my way to her bed."

He closed his eyes tightly, for just a moment, then opened them again. "She had this little-girl bed, the kind with a white wrought-iron frame." He nodded toward his hand. "You can see the pattern there, on the back of my hand. But that happened later, after the flames spread to the bed. I was with her by then."

Rising stiffly to his feet, he moved away from Elise. "I knew she was dead. As soon as I got there, I knew. I sensed it. But I couldn't just leave her there to burn. I couldn't do that to her.

"You can't imagine . . . I never expected it would be so hard, trying to lift her. Without her help, without her holding on—" He broke off and cleared his throat. "The smoke was so thick, I couldn't breathe, and the fire had already reached the bed. But I just couldn't leave her there."

He stood with his back to Elise, so she couldn't see his face and the emotion it revealed. Still kneeling where he had left her, Elise was overcome, tears running silently down her face, her arms wrapped tightly around her waist.

"You accused me of holding parts of myself sacrosanct," he said quietly, "but it wasn't a conscious thing. Paula's death . . . That part of my life isn't easy to talk about. I told myself it wasn't necessary. Knowing the way you felt about my hand, I didn't figure you would be interested in hearing how it happened. I'm sorry if—"

"Wait a minute." She wiped the tears away with trembling hands. "Back up. What do you mean, knowing the way I felt about your hand?"

"Come on, Elise. I knew you could scarcely stand to look at it." He gave a short, harsh laugh. "Hell, I don't blame you. I can't bear the sight of it myself. Neither could my parents. They acted as if it was something I had done intentionally, to embarrass them."

"Forget your parents. But the rest . . . You thought—That's why you never touched me with your left hand," she whispered, her voice uneven. "That's why you kept it out of sight, even at home. Even around me."

The tone in her voice must have reached him. He turned, staring at her as he moved closer. "I wasn't wrong about that, Elise. Damn you, I *wasn't*. Why are you doing this? Why are you dissembling now, for heaven's sake?"

His features constricting with unconcealed anger, he stopped in front of her. Reaching out with his left hand, he laid it against the side of her face in an action that bore no resemblance to a caress. If anything, it was a mocking challenge.

"What am I supposed to do now?" she asked, her throat tight with suppressed emotion. "Shriek? Shudder? Or maybe it would be more effective, more in keeping with your opinion of me, if I vomited in disgust."

Holding his gaze, she reached up to take his hand and moved it down to press it against her throat. With her other hand she unfastened the top button of her blouse, allowing the fabric to slip even farther off her shoulder. Slowly she moved his hand down until it covered her exposed breast. His swift intake of breath barely registered as she held his hand tightly against her flesh.

"I never, *never* thought it was repulsive," she whispered hoarsely. "It was simply a part of you, like your crazy midnight eyes and the muscle beside your mouth that twitches when something annoys you. I wish you had told me about it. I wish you had told me a long time ago."

He didn't respond. He was silently, intently staring at the scarred hand that was pressed against her pale, smooth flesh. In the next moment, as they both watched, he moved his hand, cupping her breast, lifting it, testing the nipple with rough strokes of his twisted thumb.

Her breath caught in her throat, her head dropping back, her eyes drifting shut. Vaguely, from a distance, she heard him mutter, "*Yes*," in a short, harsh breath, and her mind echoed the word, every inch of her body screaming it out.

Something was happening between them,

something she hadn't intended or expected but had no power—

"Garrick. Garrick, where are you?"

The fingers on her breast tightened painfully when Charis's voice, sharp and breathless, reached them from somewhere close by. Seconds later they heard Max as well.

"Do you have to screech?" he said in an exasperated tone. "You're going to give every small animal in the area a heart attack. Judas priest, Charis, they're not lost. If anyone's lost, we are."

In the next moment Charis's voice, the words incomprehensible, started low before swelling to a series of piercing soprano shrieks, then came the sound of a sharp slap, followed by dead silence.

Seven

By the time Charis and Max pushed through the foliage, the blond had recovered enough to start her wailing protests.

"Don't ever leave me alone with him again," she said, rushing toward Garrick. "I mean it, Garrick. I have never in my life been subjected to such calculated cruelty, such inhumane—He threatened to tie me to a tree!"

Ignoring his companion, Max moved closer to Elise, his eyes trained on her face. "What's up?" he asked.

Elise glanced away from his probing gaze and waved a hand toward the stream. "I found water."

"So I see."

Max didn't press her this time, but Elise could feel the power of his curiosity, then and later, after he and Charis had refreshed themselves in the cool water.

In a way Max's intense interest helped. It kept her from thinking too much about how intently Garrick was watching her. His gaze now was as earnest and unflinching as it had been when she'd held his hand against her breast. And she wasn't able to read what was in his dark eyes now any more than she had then. But when she let down her guard, she was too aware of the incredible heat of his gaze.

When they all started back toward the clearing, Max clasped Elise's hand tightly, holding her back so that the other two moved on ahead.

"Are you all right?" he asked quietly.

She glanced at him in irritation. "I wish you would stop taking my emotional temperature every time you see me. I'm fine."

"Sure you are," he said, his voice skeptical. "Knock it off, Ellie. I may not be a regular Quiz Kid, but it doesn't take a genius to figure out that Goldilocks and I walked in on something a few minutes ago." When she didn't respond, he shook his head. "Okay, be stubborn. I'm just trying to figure out what's going on."

Don't feel lonely, she thought, her lips twisting in a wry smile.

"If you hadn't told me about all the stuff your private detective came up with," he continued, "I would never have pegged Garrick as Charis's lover. I mean, he doesn't exactly drool when they're together, does he?"

Pushing a strand of hair from her face, she

shook her head in exasperation. "All right . . . all right!" she ground out. "Sweet Pete, you'd drive a saint round the bend. Don't you think I've noticed how he is around her? So maybe I had it wrong. I don't mean about the affair. I mean, maybe I was mistaken about the importance of the affair. It never occurred to me that it could have been nothing more than a . . . a . . . "

"A roll in the hay?" Max offered.

"A fling," she substituted repressively. "Strictly for illicit entertainment. Garrick might never have intended our relationship to end. Maybe this thing with Charis wasn't supposed to replace our marriage. Maybe it was supposed to be in addition to it."

"You don't sound particularly pleased at the thought of him not being in love with Charis."

It took Elise a moment to gather her thoughts together, and even then she wasn't sure she could give Max an adequate explanation.

"I wish you could see him in court," she began finally. "Garrick is— He has such a rock-solid belief in justice and truth. The first time I watched him fighting for one of his clients—" She shook her head. "I don't think I've ever respected anyone as much. And because I had such great respect for him, I automatically assumed this affair meant he had fallen in love. It never occurred to me he might take infidelity for granted. He might expect me to take it for granted as well."

"And you can't?" When she met his eyes, he said, "No, of course you can't."

Max was right. She couldn't.

She only wished she could remember when she was close to Garrick, she thought as they caught up with the other two. She wished she could remember it when he touched her.

The stranded quartet spent most of the morning watching for search planes, each with varying degrees of intensity. For Elise, the search was earnest but not desperate. Something inside her—she wasn't sure if it was nerve or ego—knew beyond doubt they would be rescued.

The strength emanating from Garrick was another factor that kept despair at bay. And how could she view the situation with any degree of sobriety when Max went around singing the theme from *Gilligan's Island*?

The strangest part of the whole thing was the isolation. To look up and see nothing in the sky except clouds and an occasional bird left her with a peculiar feeling. In Dallas, at any given moment she could have spotted five or six airplanes flying overhead. But here, where the absence of pollution made the sky seem even larger, there was nothing.

She felt somewhat like a child who couldn't quite believe school was being held even on the days she was home sick. Surely civilization ceased to exist when she was absent.

With no telephones ringing, no appointments to keep, time gained weight, each minute growing fat and sluggish, weighing them down.

Then, shortly before noon, Charis spotted a high-flying airliner and tried frantically to signal it by waving a silk scarf over her head, much to the amusement of Max. His laughter made the blond pound on him, screaming. Her outburst surprised no one, of course. In less than twenty-four hours Charis had lost control so often, Elise and Max had started playing even-odd to see who would deal with her. The result was that the blond flinched every time either of them so much as twitched.

After lunch Garrick announced he would make another try at repairing the radio, so Elise was left alone with the wrangling, but adorable, duo.

"Coward," she muttered, staring at Garrick's retreating back.

Max, quiet for once, rested his chin on one knee as he read a paperback book he had brought with him. On his other side, Charis reclined against a boulder, fanning herself with a magazine, her movements short, agitated. Occasionally she would glance at Elise or Max, as though annoyed that they weren't agitated as well.

"What are you reading?" the blond finally asked Max, breaking the silence.

He glanced up. "True crime. It's called *Blood Beneath the Elms*. You probably remember the case. After a small group gets stranded in the woods, a homicidal maniac stalks them and murders them one by one. It's pretty good."

He pulled himself up straighter, his movements

awkward because of his leg. "The interesting part is," he continued, "before he kills them, he starts cutting them up with an electric knife . . . extra-thin slices, deli-style . . . and then he saves their knuckles in these little zip-lock bags. Want to read it when I get through?"

Elise turned her head slowly to look at Max. "Can I see that?" she asked, smiling sweetly.

When he handed it to her, she bopped him on the head with it then gave it back to him. "Now, when Charis stops screaming, you can apologize to her."

Later, as she checked the swelling on Max's leg, Elise studied his face. "You're enjoying this, aren't you?"

"Being stranded?"

"Everything. The plane going down, being lost in the woods, trying to send Charis over the edge. You're enjoying the whole thing."

"There are four of us," he said. "We already have a designated whiner—and may I say she's doing a bang-up job. We have our stoic leader. And we have you, our sensitive yet robust ombudsman." He shrugged. "Getting a kick out of the whole thing was the only position left open."

After swatting him again with his book, Elise returned to what she now thought of as *her* rock and began to consider the changes in them Garrick had said isolation would bring.

The change in Charis was the most obvious. She was no longer the shy little girl she had been the day before. Even without the screaming attacks, the blond was giving a superior imitation of Elizabeth Taylor in *Who's Afraid of Virginia Woolf?*

Max, on the other hand, had definitely regressed. He had turned into the fiendish little boy she had known back on Weiden Street.

And Elise herself? Max had cast her in the role of mediator, some kind of peacemaker. Apparently he hadn't looked closely enough to see the changes in her. When the plane went down, when they lost touch with the world, the pretense she had been living for most of her adult life had suddenly seemed foolish.

She had shed that part of herself, her superficial manner, the way an animal sheds its winter coat. It was of no use to her out here. Things that had seemed vitally important suddenly had no meaning. Emotions and instincts, basic and primitive passions she had buried long ago because she didn't know how to deal with them, were coming to the surface without her consent.

The only one who seemed not to have undergone a metamorphosis was Garrick. Although earlier he had forced himself to open up to her, he was still tactful . . . and withdrawn. He continued to observe all the polite rules, while refusing to give in to tension or fear. It was, of course, what she expected from him, exactly. Above all, Garrick was a civilized man.

After giving the instrument panel one last thump, Garrick leaned back in the pilot seat.

The radio was useless, beyond repair. He had figured as much, but had decided to give it one more try, just in case.

Just in case of what? he asked himself with mocking humor. Just in case it healed itself overnight?

He ran a restless hand through his hair. He wasn't in the cockpit to repair the radio, so there was no use trying to fool himself. He was there because he needed time alone to think. Thinking wasn't something he did well around Elise. For example, this morning at the stream. He hadn't been thinking then. If he could have managed even a moment's thought, he wouldn't have left her with the idea he was trying to put the make on her.

For once he had been reaching her. They were talking, dammit. They were actually communicating. He could have used that to establish some kind of base, a point from which they could progress.

But he had blown it. When she took his hand and held it to her breast, he had stopped thinking of communication. He could only think of how good it felt to touch her again.

Why had she done it? Why had she held his hand, pressed it so intimately to her breast? The ready explanation was, she had done it out of pity, and the emotion he'd read in her green eyes was only compassion.

The thought ripped him up. He didn't want such a hateful, puny emotion from her. He would rather she was repulsed by him than feel pity for him.

Suddenly he refused to accept his own explanation. It had to be more than pity. It had to! And, if some deeper, stronger emotions were there, he was determined to ferret them out . . . use them.

An hour later, when he joined the others, Garrick was calm and steady again. He knew now what he had to do.

Max turned his head as Garrick sat near him. "What do you think? Any hope for the radio?"

He shook his head. "Deceased."

Charis groaned and hid her face with her hands. Elise's expression didn't change, as though she had expected his news. Max stared at his hands for a moment, then began spinning a wild yarn about their lives as greasy-haired savages, all of them wearing leopard-skin teddies.

Garrick knew what Max was up to. It had taken him awhile to figure Max out, but now he realized that Elise's friend pulled out his clown act whenever he felt the atmosphere was becoming too tense, whenever he thought the others needed to get their minds off their situation.

Garrick tuned back in to the conversation just as Elise was offering her own extravagant version of their future.

"If we have to be stranded for twenty or thirty years," she said, "I prefer to think we'll be the originators of a secret, advanced civilization, something like Atlantis, or that one in the old

Tarzan movie, the one that was ruled by a beautiful, statuesque woman."

Garrick smiled. "Since you happen to be the only statuesque woman here, I take it you're running for queen."

Max shot her a suspicious look. "Wait a minute, I remember that movie. All the regular people had to work like dogs to keep the witchy woman in jewels and silk togas, and they kept dropping flat on their faces every time she sauntered into a room."

Elise casually brushed a bit of dried leaf from her sleeve. "Works for me," she said.

Diving toward her, Max swept her into a headlock and rubbed his knuckles across the top of her head as she shouted with laughter.

The moment Max touched Elise, Garrick's amusement died a cold death. Just seconds earlier he had decided he might grow to like Max after all. Now, he had to shove his fists into his pockets to keep from strangling the man.

He wanted to feel Max's neck under his fingers. He wanted to pick Max up off the ground and shake him until he agreed to keep his damn hands off Elise.

Throughout the rest of the evening, Elise watched Garrick without looking at him directly. Although his mood had been strangely charged since their encounter that morning beside the stream, Garrick's behavior changed even more after he returned from the plane. The banked force seemed to grow and swell around him. It made her and the other two tread warily around him.

In certain ways, though, Charis acted differently from her and Max, Elise observed. The longer Charis went without her cigarettes, the more difficult she became, nagging and whining and complaining, sometimes under her breath, sometimes at the top of her lungs. As they sat around the campfire that evening, Elise almost wished Charis would become hysterical so she would have an excuse to sock her.

". . . supposed to make everything all right. That's what men are for. You and Elise's dimwitted Max should be taking better care of me . . . nothing to eat and the water tastes like bad fish. If I don't get a cigarette soon, I'm going to do something dreadful. I promise I will. Why haven't they found us? There should be hundreds of planes out looking for us. My parents are such idiots, they probably don't even know I'm missing. My father, speaking of dimwits, even if he knew, wouldn't be able to do anything about it. I've never seen a more inept, impotent man. All my life, he's—"

"I thought both your parents were dead," said Garrick, staring hard at her.

Charis glanced up, her eyes wide and startled. "I— The thing is, you see—" She shook her head, as though trying to rearrange her thoughts. "I had an argument with my parents . . . years ago, a terrible argument. You wouldn't believe how cruel they were to me,

Garrick. So, well, I just decided that they were no longer my parents. In my mind, they were dead."

Elise, without looking up, said, "Is your sister, Phyllis, also dead in your mind?"

"You know my sister?"

Elise smiled and shook her head. "No, someone happened to mention her. I merely wonder how you see her."

"Phyllis hates me." Meeting Garrick's gaze, Charis sent him a pleading smile. "When the real world is cruel, sometimes it helps to make up a fantasy world, a world that's kind. You understand, don't you?"

Garrick shifted his gaze away from her. "We all deal with our problems in different ways," he said quietly. "How you deal with yours is your business—and only yours."

Elise stared at him, studying his face. He hadn't known. He hadn't lied to her about Charis having no family. Oh, there had been other lies, but at least she could cross one off, she thought with an emotion strangely like relief.

Feeling the tension in the air, Elise decided it was time to change the subject. She cleared her throat noisily and leaned back against her boulder. "Have you ever seen so many stars?" she asked pleasantly.

Max shot a glance at the sky. "That's because there aren't any city lights to dim them. Out here, you can see why people down through the ages have looked to the stars for aid and comfort. Stars led the way to the Christ Child, they told men's fortunes and predicted their downfall. It was the color of a star that whispered the secret of an expanding universe to astronomers."

"Poets have certainly gotten a lot of mileage out of them," Garrick said. "Shakespeare especially. A quote sticks in my mind. . . ." Slowly he turned his head and met Elise's gaze across the campfire. "'That I should love a bright particular star,'" he said, his voice husky.

His eyes, darker than midnight, reached deep inside her, twisting her, turning her, pulling her body toward him. In a replay of the day they met, she was lost in the depths of his eyes. As she had then, she felt her breasts heave in reaction and heat spread through her.

But, in an abrupt movement, Garrick broke eye contact and continued speaking, as though nothing out of the ordinary had happened.

"It was Shakespeare's way of illustrating a truly hopeless love," he said. "According to him, you have to be satisfied with standing in the distant radiance because, being trapped on earth, you can never hope to get close to the real brilliance, the real warmth, a star generates."

She barely heard him. She was still reeling from the silent conversation that had passed between them moments before.

Jeez, Louise, I'm sweating, she thought as she ran a shaking hand across her face.

It seemed to take forever for her breathing to return to normal, but when she once again gave her attention to the conversation around her, Garrick and Max were still talking about isolation, while Charis continued to mutter under her breath, chanting her need for a cigarette.

"Remember the show we saw on TV when we were kids, Max?" Elise asked a moment later. "You and Annie came over to watch television because Daddy was working late one night. It was a science-fiction movie about a couple who went to the top of the Empire State Building. While they were up there, some kind of weird fog moved in, obscuring the world below. I don't remember what happened next, but for some reason they had to walk all the way down to street level."

"The elevators wouldn't work," Max said, "I always figured the fog ate the cables."

"And when they finally reached street level," said Elise, pointedly ignoring him, "there was no one there. Everyone, every person on earth, had disappeared."

"The fog ate them," Max said. "Why are you reminding me of this sweet little story when I don't have my book to swat you with? What's your point?"

When she laughed and shook her head, Garrick said, "The characters in the show left the world behind when they went to the top of the building. And when they left it behind—or maybe *because* they left it behind—it disappeared. Elise is saying she feels as though her presence in the world was what kept it going. And she's wondering if her feeling is an indication of some hidden conceit she should be trying to root out of herself."

"Very good, Counselor," she said acknowledging his accurate reading. "So what's your verdict?"

"I find you guilty of being human."

"Oh no, not that," Max gasped.

Elise cautiously met Garrick's gaze. "You feel it too?"

He shrugged. "Our perception of the world is purely subjective. It's the only way it can be. There isn't a general pool of thought or emotion we can plug into. Every signal goes into an exclusive unit, the brain, for processing. So the world as you see it or I see it is inextricably bound to one particular mind. Move the brain's storage tank—the individual—to another location, and because the brain no longer perceives it, the world ceases to exist."

He smiled. "Which is a long-winded way of saying we are each the center of our own universe."

"If the world still is out there, why hasn't it found us yet?" Max asked.

Garrick smiled and shook his head. "I've been thinking about that stream. It could go underground at some point, but chances are, it empties into something larger. A lake or a river."

Suddenly Max sat up straighter. "Damned if I don't think you're right. And if you find either of those things, you're going to find people, sure as hell. We should at least give it a shot."

"Give it a shot?" Elise said. "You mean follow the stream?"

Max nodded. "I mean stick with it and find out where it goes."

"I think Max has the right idea," Garrick said quietly. "One of us should start out first thing in the morning and follow the stream to its outlet."

"Let Max go," Charis said, her voice sulky. "If he meets any wild animals, he can irritate them to death."

Garrick looked at Max. "The leg is giving you some pain, isn't it? A fractured bone?"

Max nodded. "That's what I figure."

Elise glanced sharply at her friend, noticing for the first time the deep lines around his eyes and mouth. "Why didn't you tell me?" she demanded.

"What would you have done, kissed it better?"

"So I guess that leaves me," Garrick said softly.

Max had been staring into the fire, but now he looked up and met Garrick's gaze. Elise watched in bewilderment as some kind of silent, male communication took place. After a moment Garrick moved his head slightly, almost but not quite a nod, as though he were answering a silent question from Max.

"There really should be two," said Max, staring again into the fire. "That way if one gets hurt, the other can go for help. My leg isn't hurting that bad. I'll—"

"You'll stay here and stay off that leg," Elise said. "You're right about two going, but I'm the logical choice. The robust type, remember?"

"I don't know, Elise—" Max began.

"It's settled," she said firmly as she rose to her feet. "And if we're going to start out tomorrow, we'd better all get to bed."

Garrick decided he would stay behind for a while, but Max and Charis both followed Elise to the plane. Inside the Cessna Max shot a glance at her, rolling his eyes in exasperation as he listened to Charis.

"Doesn't she ever stop?" he muttered.

The blond's head jerked up sharply. "Stop talking about me. Stop talking at all. I hate you."

"There's news," he said.

"I don't want to stay here with you," Charis continued. "Garrick should be the one to stay. He's crippled. He has a deformed hand." She shuddered. "Have you seen it? I hate it when he takes it out of his pocket. I've always had a delicate stomach, and the sight of it makes me queasy."

Elise felt as though she had taken a fist in her solar plexus. Anger, violent and unyielding, exploded inside her. Seconds later she was moving across the plane on her knees, heading toward Charis.

Giving a squeak of surprise, Charis began scooting backward. "Leave me alone. The only reason you're so mad is because Garrick and I are having an affair and . . . and I don't see why I should be punished because your husband prefers me."

"Way to go, Goldilocks," said Max, his voice bland. "That ought to calm her down."

"I didn't mean anything," Charis whimpered as she tried to hide behind Max. "It's . . . it's nicotine withdrawal."

"As an excuse, that's wearing pretty thin," Max said. "You might try a chemical imbalance or PMS, but I don't think Elise is going to buy either of those."

"Stop hiding," Elise said through tight, white lips. She reached around and dragged Charis from behind Max. "Don't you *ever* talk about Garrick's hand. Don't even talk about it. You couldn't possibly know what people like you have done to him with your small-mindedness, your stupidity."

Charis shook loose of her grasp. "Don't tell me what to do! Just leave me *alone*!"

When the blond reached out and slapped her, Elise almost laughed. "You call that a slap? That wet-noodle tap?"

Charis, obviously expecting Elise to react with anger, seemed stunned. But she didn't remain stunned for long. Spitting and scratching, she flew at Elise and was on top of her before the latter knew what was happening. With only a little effort Elise rolled over and held the blond down, dodging her flailing fists.

"Cat fight!" Max called through cupped fingers. "Cat fight!"

Elise jerked her head up and pinned him with a look. "I can't believe you said those words. They're beneath you, Max Decatur. You've never had a sexist bone in your body. What on earth has gotten into—"

Her breath left her in a whoosh when Charis kneed her in the stomach and scrambled upright, punching Elise in the shoulder with both fists. Charis was raging, hitting Elise again and again . . . with no effect whatsoever.

As Elise stared down at the blond, one dark brow raised, the whole episode suddenly struck her as utterly ridiculous. She started to chuckle, and before long her body shook with uncontrollable laughter.

Charis blinked twice, staring at Elise's open amusement. "Stop laughing!" she shouted, but her lips began to twitch at the corners. "I wasn't through fighting," she said as she landed yet another weak blow to Elise's shoulder.

Seconds later she was leaning against Elise, taking air in through her nose in loud, snorting laughter.

"That wasn't bad for amateurs," Max said when their yelps of laughter had dwindled to giggles. "But next time we need to find a mud puddle so you can—" He broke off when both women tossed shoes at him.

"Hey, I know when I'm not wanted," he said, throwing up his hands. "No one has to knock Max Decatur in the head with a shoe. I'll go join old Gary . . . talk about man stuff . . . do some bonding." He was still muttering when he got out of the plane.

Garrick glanced up when Max joined him, but quickly returned his gaze to the dying fire.

"They threw me out," said Max, hobbling over to a rock on the other side of the campfire. "I wanted to talk to you anyway." He hesitated, as though uncertain of how to continue.

"If you're worried about Elise," Garrick said

quietly, "don't be. I'll take of her." He looked Max squarely in the eye. "Why did you go along with me? Why did you maneuver Elise into coming with me tomorrow?"

It was a moment before Max spoke, and when he did, his tone was more serious than Garrick had ever heard it. "Elise thinks your relationship is over, but several things have led me to believe there are still unanswered questions. I've spent a lot of years, too many years, with unanswered questions. I don't want that for her. If the two of you are alone, maybe she can work out the unresolved stuff and be finished with you for good . . . or not."

Garrick turned back to stare at the glowing embers. "What makes you think she's not already finished with me?"

"A lot of things. One was that look you two shared across the campfire," Max said lazily. "I could have jump-started a 747 on the current running between you two."

Garrick didn't respond. No response was necessary. He had no doubt the electricity between him and Elise was obvious to anyone who was paying attention.

"I've noticed something too," Garrick said after a while. "Every time this girl Annie's name is mentioned, you get a look in your eyes, one I can't read. Was she someone important? Someone who left you with all those unanswered questions?"

Max gave a harsh laugh. "You could say that. She was my wife. The most important person in my life. Until she skipped town with my brother. That was over ten years ago."

"And it's still driving you crazy. After all these years." Garrick drew in a tight, painful breath. "That's not something I wanted to hear. I wanted to believe that eventually the pain dulls." He paused, rubbing his throbbing temple with two fingers. "If you saw her again, if out of the blue she appeared before you, how would you feel? Do you think, after all this time and after what she did to you, you would still be attracted to her physically?"

It was quite a while before Max answered. "I've asked myself the same question a million times. What would happen if, after all this time, I suddenly ran into her? I think I would try to kill her. I would try to strangle the lying, cheating life out of her, but—" He shook his head.

"But even as you strangled her," Garrick continued for him, his voice filled with instinctive knowledge, "even as you hated her, you would be wanting her. And of the two emotions, desire would be the stronger."

Max gave a short, abrupt nod. "I guess there are some things time doesn't cure."

Drawing in a rough breath, Garrick stood up and kicked dirt at the last of the coals. "That's what I was afraid of."

He hadn't wanted to hear it, didn't want to believe it, but he knew instantly it was the truth. No matter what had happened between him and Elise, no matter what kind of time and distance came between them, he would want her with the last breath he took.

Eight

"Do your feet hurt?" Ducking a branch, Elise did a quick skip-hop to catch up with Garrick. "Why didn't you force me to keep up my exercising after I quit modeling?"

"Force you?" he called back. "You're kidding, right?"

She laughed. "All right, so I'm the captain of my ship and all that jazz. But still, my feet hurt." It was early afternoon of the second day since they had left the others behind. The night just past had been spent in an old abandoned deer stand, a partially decomposed wooden box perched atop four rickety posts. She hadn't been sure she wanted to climb the wooden ladder that moved under her feet with each step. But when Garrick reminded her it was either the deer stand or the ground—and that on the ground was where slithery, crawly things usually chose to sleep—she decided the deer stand looked perfectly safe. Once in it, she found she was too exhausted to worry, too exhausted, in fact, to stay awake.

Today they seemed to be making better time than they had the day before. There were places where the going was rough, places along the bank where the brush grew too thickly for them to push through. When they encountered one of these obstructions, they had to find a way around it. A couple of times they almost lost the stream, but even with the detours, they must have traveled at least fifteen miles from where the plane went down.

From the moment they had left the others, Garrick had been in a strange mood. He seemed more relaxed than she had seen him in a long time, almost lighthearted at times. She should have been relieved by the change, but something about him made her watchful.

It could have been nothing more than the way he was dressed. His navy-blue T-shirt and black jeans weren't anything out of the ordinary, but combined with the handkerchief he had tied around his forehead to keep the perspiration out of his eyes and the small pack he had slung across his back, the total effect was somewhat intimidating.

Elise kept watching him. Yesterday she told herself he hadn't changed. Now, she wasn't so sure. Because his clothes weren't the only difference. There was something about the way he moved, something about the way he held his head in an ever-vigilant attitude.

"Why are you so quiet?" he asked, pausing for a moment. "You were talking nonstop an hour ago, now suddenly you're dead silent. You haven't got a gun trained on my back, have you?"

She laughed and reached down to scratch her leg. "I was just thinking that you look different somehow. A little primitive." She tilted her head, studying his face with the red kerchief across his brow. "But still civilized. A noble savage maybe. Or the prototype of man."

He raised one thick brow. "I think the sun's beginning to get to you. I'll have you know I'm nothing less than the culmination of centuries of advancing civilization."

"Well, I know, silly. But that stuff's in your head. And it wasn't your head I've been staring at all afternoon," she said, giving one hard buttock a swift pat as she walked past him.

He twisted around to look behind him, then caught up with her in two long strides. "Getting playful, are we? Why don't you take the lead so I can admire the view? Have I told you how glad I am you decided to wear as few clothes as possible?"

"I didn't dress to please or to tease you. And it's a good thing I decided on this," she said, indicating her khaki shorts and white tank top, "because it's getting hotter every minute. I guess I shouldn't complain though. In March, in this part of the country, we could as easily have snow as these high temperatures."

Walking side by side, they continued to discuss the weather until he decided he should move ahead to clear a path through some briars. Only when he had gone several yards did it occur to Elise what had been going on minutes earlier. They had been flirting!

She and her estranged almost-ex-husband, the man who had grown so cold and distant lately, had been flirting. The realization brought a spurt of startled laughter from her.

An hour later, when she and Garrick stopped to rest, she sat soaking her feet in the cool water of the stream and still couldn't believe it. Perhaps they flirted because of the weird mood he was in, she told herself, certain she wouldn't, couldn't be daring enough to instigate it.

She glanced back at Garrick, leaning against a tree. "What do you think? Any signs of humanity yet?"

"In you? I'd say you're coming along fairly well."

She scooped up a handful of water and threw it at him. When only the last flicked drops reached him, he laughed. "You've got a good aim, so I wouldn't throw anything more substantial than water if I were you."

She raised one slender brow in haughty inquiry. "Is that a threat?"

He laughed again and shook his head. "I haven't seen anything. No Styrofoam cups or beer cans floating in the water. No Big Mac cartons or bubble-gum wrappers or cigarette packages. That means either we're still not getting close to people, or else the people around here are exceptionally neat. I'd say the first is the more likely choice."

"A Big Mac," she said, her voice wistful as she ignored everything else he had said. "What I wouldn't give for a burger right now." She sighed. "Oh well, I guess I can wait. But if we spot any golden arches, you just better not get in my way. I'll be sweet-talking one of those guys behind the counter so fast, it'll make your head spin." She patted the pockets of her shorts. "Why didn't I think of bringing money?"

"Don't worry. Sweet-talking will get the job done just fine." He gave a rueful laugh. "I don't think you realize how you draw people. You can't see the inner radiance in you that pulls people toward you, all different kinds of people, sophisticated or down-to-earth." He paused. "Max is in love with you."

Her head jerked around. She stared at him in astonishment before vehemently shaking her head in denial.

Max? she thought. For a second she considered the possibility that her dear friend could be the one who waited to love her. For one brief moment she allowed the idea into her heart, but the only thing she felt was disappointment. No, it wasn't Max.

"You're wrong," she said slowly. "Max is the closest thing I'll ever have to a brother. He loves me, but he's not in love with me. Our friend Annie burned that kind of love out of him when she left him. He's simply not capable of it anymore." She smiled. "And even if he were, it wouldn't work. We would kill each other within a week. No," she said more softly, "Max isn't the one."

Rising abruptly to his feet, Garrick turned away from her. "I'm going to look around for a while. You rest, soak your feet in the stream." He removed the handkerchief from his head and tossed it to her. "You can dampen this for me while you're at it."

Once again his mood had shifted. He had sounded angry that she couldn't see Max as anything but a friend. Shaking her head, she wondered if she would ever understand him.

Resting her elbows on her knees, she stared longingly at the water. It was too shallow to do any good. Even if she lay down in it, she would only succeed in soaking her back. She supposed if she rolled over and over, wallowing like a pig in a mud puddle, she might be able to get wet all over.

Closing her eyes, she pictured the pool in the backyard of their Dallas home. It was lined with shiny, cobalt-blue tile that made the water look cool and inviting no matter what the temperature.

She sat in the wilderness, her feet in the stream, and made a mental list of all the things she would give up for one dip in that cool blue swimming pool. The list had gotten rather unwieldy by the time Garrick finally returned.

"Where have you been? You've been gone almost half an hour."

He grinned. "I was out doing pioneer stuff while my woman beat my Fruit of the Looms on a rock."

"What is it?" she asked suspiciously. "You've got a very strange look in your eyes. You're up to something."

"I have a surprise for you," he said, reaching down to pull her to her feet.

When she had slipped back into her sandals, she followed Garrick through bushes and under low-hanging trees, and after a while he turned toward the stream.

Minutes later he held back a flowering shrub, letting her go first. And there it was. A tiny, rock-lined pool. The water wasn't exactly blue, but it was close enough. It would do.

Garrick watched the look of astonished pleasure spread across her features. Seconds later she began to run toward the pool, disposing of her shoes and the khaki shorts as she went. By the time she reached the water, she wore only the white tank top and her white silk panties. She let out a rebel yell as she jumped in, her arms up, her head thrown back in abandonment.

As he watched, he felt the wildness of her pulling at him, beckoning him, seducing his senses. Excitement quickened his blood. He wanted this woman. *This* woman. The woman he had just missed knowing.

When she called his name, motioning with

one hand for him to join her, he finally managed to move, stripping down to his underwear before diving in.

The water was wonderful. Pure joy. The blue-tiled pool back home had never felt so wonderful—because back home, Elise had never been in such desperate need of a swim. Back home, getting hot and tired and sweaty were forbidden, high on the list of things that would get you kicked out of the country club.

For over an hour, she and Garrick splashed and yelled and ducked each other like kids, reveling in the feel of the dust washing off their bodies.

But too soon it was time to leave, time to get on with their quest.

On the bank she found a cottonwood tree that leaned out across the creek, only four feet off the ground, and rested against it as she shook the water from her long hair.

"It shouldn't take us long to dry off," Garrick said.

Then, in a move that took her by surprise, he ran his fingers down her bare arm, wiping the moisture away.

The instant he touched her, desire shook through her, hardening her nipples. The wet fabric of her tank top clung to her breasts, hiding nothing.

Garrick slowly lowered his gaze, sucking in a sharp breath when he saw the changes in her body. As though he were in a trance, as though he had no will of his own, he reached out to her, running his index finger across one taut peak, then the other.

"You need me, Elise," he ground out hoarsely. "You need me as much as I need you."

When her only response was to shake her head restlessly, he stepped closer. "You're a healthy, sensual woman, Elise, with a healthy, sensual appetite. It can't have been easy for you," he whispered, "going without lovemaking for this length of time."

"I can handle it," she said, her lips tight as she avoided his gaze.

"Why should you have to? Why should either of us have to? When we get back, you'll start divorce proceedings. It will all be over. Don't you think we should make the most of the time we have left?"

Pushing away from the tree, she took two steps away from him. "You're crazy."

"Am I?" Grasping her shoulder, he pulled her back against him, moving his hips so that her buttocks fit tight against his hard thighs.

"Tell me you don't want me," he said. "Tell me you don't want . . . this."

When his fingers moved between her thighs, she tried to tell herself she wanted him to stop, that she wanted him to stay away from her. But she began to move restlessly against the hand, effectively putting an end to the lies. She didn't want him to stop. She didn't ever want him to stop.

Swinging around, she threw her arms around his neck and pulled his lips down to hers, opening her mouth to him, sucking his tongue deep inside. Hunger had wiped out memory. Greedy desire had wiped out sanity.

Grasping her buttocks with both hands, he lifted her up, settling her on the cottonwood, and seconds later he was fitting himself between the smooth thighs that had opened for him. He pressed against her, then moved away, then returned the pressure, teasing her into a wildness she had never felt before, never thought to feel.

She was still calling him crazy when she pushed her shirt up and pulled his head down to her breasts. Still calling him crazy as he licked the moisture from her nipples and from between her breasts. She repeated the words over and over when he lifted her again, stripped her panties off, then entered her with one hard thrust. But Elise no longer knew what the words meant. They came automatically, the same way she automatically wrapped her long legs around him. And the litany seemed a part of the primitive passion ripping her apart as each new thrust of his body came harder and faster and wilder than the last.

"Witchy woman," he muttered before groaning one last time as he lifted her to carry her, legs still wrapped around him, to the grass beneath the tree. "Max was right. You're a witch."

His hands were all over her, both hands, and there was just enough awareness left in her for her to cry out in sheer joy. Throwing her head back, she felt her eyelids began to drift down as the sensations rocked through her, weakening her.

"No! Don't close your eyes," he said, his voice unexpectedly harsh. "See me, Elise. This time I want you to see *me* when we make love."

She didn't understand, and she couldn't focus her thoughts long enough even to try to understand, but she did as he bid her. If he had told her to kneel and kiss his feet, she would have done it. Anything to hold on to the delirious pleasure-pain that his touch was bringing to her body.

It seemed only seconds later when her back arched, thrusting her upward. Her green eyes were wide and unfocused as spasm after spasm ripped through her body, bringing a release so intense, so complete, it almost left her senseless.

Through the vibrating red haze settling around her, she heard him call her name. Just once. A high, keening sound that brought to mind vast wilderness and the cry of a lone wolf.

For a long time afterward they lay with their arms around each other, her body half on, half off his. The white tank top was still pushed high on her chest, because at the time neither had had the patience to remove it, and now Elise was too dazed to move, too lazy to care.

"Good Lord," he said in a rough whisper, "you needed that, didn't you?"

"Oh please," she said, still trying to catch her

breath, "can't you tell when a woman is faking it?"

Laughter began deep in his chest and rumbled to the surface, shaking her as she lay in his arms, taking them both by surprise.

And suddenly they were both laughing, and neither could seem to stop. They held on to each other and rolled in the grass, laughing. They were like two people who had lost their minds. Or the inhibitions society had forced upon them.

It was a while later when Garrick sat up and stared down at her. "I guess I'd better go back and find our clothes and the food," he said.

So sensible, she thought with a smile. Even here, he couldn't quite shed his civilized nature—or was it a *practical* nature?

After he had left her, Elise lay back on the grass, thinking of him, feeling the leftover glow, remembering again the wonder she had felt when he had unintentionally, instinctively touched her with his scarred hand. It made her feel a closeness to him that hadn't been there in—

Elise sat up, and every thought fled as a terrible realization struck her. A truth so strong, it almost made her double over.

She had been so confident that she felt nothing for Garrick except desire. But it was a lie. She had lied to Max, and worse, she had lied to herself. She had loved Garrick the moment she'd first seen him—and she had never stopped loving him.

And the unnamed emotion, the thing inside herself that she hadn't been able to look at, was deep, devastating pain. Pain caused by his betrayal.

She loved him. More now than in the beginning. And he had betrayed her.

She almost could see him touching Charis, giving his mistress the pleasure he had just given his wife. The pleasure that should not—did not!—belong to anyone but her.

A savage sound, a combination of grief and anger, came from deep in her throat. She was choking on rage as she pounded the ground with her fists.

Seconds later she felt his arms around her, holding her hands still, pulling her close.

"Elise, what is it? Stop struggling. Talk to me. What's wrong?"

She jerked one hand free and slammed it into his shoulder. "You *bastard!*" She spat out the words. "You made me feel again. I had shut it off. I thought watching my life fall apart didn't hurt. But you made me feel again. Why couldn't you have left me alone? Why couldn't you let me go on fooling myself into believing none of it mattered."

Pulling away from him, she scooted away, her movements born of desperation. "I hate you. Damn your cold, callous, civilized soul, *I hate you!*"

He grabbed her arm and jerked her closer. "Good." The word came from low in his throat. "Go ahead and hate me. It will be the most honest emotion I've gotten from you in our entire marriage."

Reaching out, he placed his scarred hand on her hip, pressing her close to him, making her aware of his arousal. "I can live with your hatred," he said in a hoarse whisper just before his mouth covered hers.

"Come on, Elise"—he spoke the words into her open mouth—"hate me some more."

His mouth slid to her throat, spreading hot kisses. Then he pushed up her breast with one hand, sucked the tip deep in his mouth. "I'm starving for it, Elise," he murmured against her soft flesh. "I'm starving for it."

This time the words she repeated as they made love were different. She told him in every way she could think of how much she hated him. And as she said the words, she tried to devour him. She tried frantically to assuage the desperate need only he created in her.

When it was over, they lay several feet apart on the grass. Again Elise felt drained, but this time it was the aftermath of a pain she couldn't shake off.

After a while, he sat up and pushed an unsteady hand through his hair, his features tight and drawn.

"Elise—" he began, breaking off when they heard, from across the stream, the sounds of dogs barking and children squealing with laughter.

The sound escaping from Elise was almost a sob. "I think we've just found civilization," she whispered.

Nine

Near the outskirts of Springfield, Missouri, a road had been cut into a hill, twisting through the trees and around giant boulders. On this late April night one limousine after another traveled the twining road, each heading for a sprawling white mansion with a ten-acre yard. Like a subdivision for giants, the white mansion with its ten-acre yard was surrounded by other mansions with ten-acre yards.

The white mansion, the destination for all the limousines, was alight from stem to stern. The winding drive glowed discreetly, the source of the illumination concealed in carefully trimmed shrubbery, looking like the fruit of some exotic, radioactive plant.

The mansion's lighting, on the other hand, wasn't at all discreet. The area in and around the house was ablaze with lights, producing artificial daylight for the lucky guests who were no less radiant than the house. They gleamed with gold, silver, precious stones, and the confidence of the privileged. The crème de la crème, these elite three hundred or so, came from all over the country to honor a woman they wouldn't have given a nod to if she hadn't been married to a man whose power equaled or surpassed their own. It was the night of Mona's birthday celebration.

Elise had thought, had hoped, that by being in a plane crash, by being stranded for three days in the wilderness, she had finally found an excuse for missing the annual event that would satisfy her mother. She should have known better. The minute Mona heard they were missing, even before she had begun to harass the authorities, she had instructed her secretary to start making calls to postpone the party until after her daughter and son-in-law were found. She never doubted they would be found, alive and well. Not even death would have the temerity to thwart Mona in celebrating her birthday.

The children that Garrick and Elise had heard at the stream had taken them to their home, almost three miles to the south. There, they had contacted the local sheriff, who had shown up with amazing speed in a battered Jeep.

Sheriff Dobbs had taken them back to the crash site to pick up Max, Charis, and the luggage. And so their adventure had ended, with no permanent damage done to any one of them. At least none that was visible.

Tonight, as Elise looked around the room, taking in the details of the glittering scene, she found it difficult to believe the days spent with Garrick in the hills were real. Had they really happened?

She was here, in Springfield, just as though there had been no interruption in her life. Just as though she and Garrick had never shared those moments of magnificent wildness beside a mountain stream.

She wouldn't think of it, she told herself—not for the first time. She had to put it all out of her mind. She had to for the sake of her own survival.

Elise had spent the past week juggling her schedule, smoothing ruffled feathers, making promises she wasn't sure she could keep. But she was here. She was here because she couldn't defy her mother.

She had spent quite a bit of time trying to decide what to wear. Her gown was long, strapless, and formfitting, as though a piece of fine red silk had been thrown around her body and stitched in place. She wore her hair down, and her bangs fell in a dramatic slash across her brow. Equally theatrical was the beaten-gold Egyptian necklace spreading across her chest and the matching earrings brushing against her shoulders when she moved.

No one at the party knew she was bluffing. She wasn't comfortable in the high-fashion costume, but she had made the effort for Mona.

Everybody gets decked out in their sexiest clothes to impress their mamas. I believe that. Sure I do, she thought.

Shut up, she told the voice in her head. She didn't want to think about Garrick . . . or that tonight she would see her husband for the first time since they'd been stranded together. She was at this party to mingle with the same people she had mingled with last year and the year before. She was here to pretend she was interested in the gossip, pretend she understood and sympathized with their self-centered tragedies and triumphs.

She was here to catch hell, she added silently as she glanced up and saw Jason and Sharon bearing down on her.

Neither of Mona's children by her first husband resembled their mother. Jason was tall and thin with a receding hairline. Sharon was also tall, but she was built like a linebacker. When they were younger, she was always hauling bullies off her older brother.

"Elise," said Jason, taking her hands as he kissed her cheek. "I can't tell you how pleased we were to hear you survived that terrible accident. We were so worried about you, weren't we, Sharon? Now, you turn up without even a scratch to show for it."

"And you wasted all that worry," said Elise, shaking her head. "Maybe next time you'll get lucky and I'll break a bone or two."

"Next time?" Jason asked skeptically. "Don't tell me you're going to fly again? What goes up always comes down. It's a law of nature."

"Have you been watching PBS again?" she asked, her voice bland, her green eyes sparkling.

"Leave him alone," Sharon said sharply. "Someone like you, practically growing up on the streets the way you did, couldn't possibly understand a man like Jason. He's sensitive to atmospheres, as all artists are."

"Artist?" Elise said. "I thought you were working on the great American novel."

"The publishing business is in the hands of fools," said Jason, lifting his chin belligerently. "The art world is much more forward-thinking."

Sharon sent Elise a smug smile. "Jason is studying with one of the greatest painters in the country."

"Is that right?" Elise murmured, one slender brow raised in inquiry as she studied her half-brother. "So you're finally going to learn how to color inside the lines."

When she heard the sound of deep laughter, Elise swung around and found Garrick standing directly behind her.

"I believe Sharon was right," he said. "You must have been raised on the streets. I know a street-fighter when I hear one." Somehow he made the words sound like a compliment. After a moment he glanced at her brother and sister. "I think Mona's looking for you two."

When Sharon and Jason left, Elise panicked. She didn't know what to say to him. It was strange seeing him in this setting. There had been so many strong emotions flowing between them the last time they were together, but maybe all those emotions had been products of the isolation. Maybe they had all been left behind in an Oklahoma wilderness.

She searched his face for any sign of the noble savage, but she found none. What she found, however, was just as devastating, just as compelling. The sight of him in a dinner jacket always made her weak. The sight of him—period—had always made her weak.

"You are the most beautiful thing I've ever seen in my life," he said. He hadn't taken his eyes off her once since he joined her. "Hello . . . I'm Garrick. I'm from Dallas."

Her throat constricted, and she swallowed with difficulty. "That's—" She coughed and began again. "That's funny, so am I."

He simply smiled.

When the silence began to make her uncomfortable, she said, "Where's your date?" She glanced around. "No man as attractive as you has to come to a party alone."

"I'm alone by choice," he murmured. "I had a feeling, a strange restless ache right around here"—he brushed a finger across his heart—"that told me I should come alone. What about you?"

She shrugged. "I had a date, but he dumped me. He dropped me like a hot rock to run off to take some silly pictures in Patagonia."

"The man's a fool. Dance with me."

Before she could say anything, before she could put him off with an excuse, she was in his arms.

This was the moment she had been dreading all evening. She had wondered how she would react when he was near, and now she knew. Nothing had changed. Dinner jacket or loin-cloth, Garrick was Garrick. And as long as there was breath in her body, she would love him.

She pulled back. She had an immediate, urgent need to get away from him, to get away from the feelings he aroused in her. "I—"

"Garrick! Elise, darling, you didn't tell me that Garrick had arrived."

At any other time the accusation in Mona's voice would have raised Elise's hackles, but not this time. This time it was exactly the interruption Elise had been looking for.

Stepping out of Garrick's arms, Elise turned to her mother. Mona née Klag Thornton Bright Charles Parker was a lean redhead who, on tiptoes, might manage to reach Elise's armpit. Although she was getting very close to sixty, there wasn't a wrinkle in Mona's paper-thin skin. No wrinkle would dare to settle on her face.

Mona had always known what she wanted, and she didn't care what she had to do to get it. At the moment what she wanted and what she had happened to coincide. She had a rich, presentable husband who didn't have the time to keep an eye on how much money his wife was spending.

"I just arrived minutes ago, Mona," said Garrick, leaning down to kiss one gaunt cheek. "And how is the birthday girl?"

Mona giggled. The effect was so startling to Elise that she almost giggled herself.

"I'm perfectly wonderful," Mona gushed. "Especially now that I see the two of you together. I knew

Elise would come to her senses sooner or later. I was telling John only yesterday that you two—"

"We were just on our way to the terrace to dance," said Garrick, interrupting her. "Out where it's not so crowded."

Taking Elise's hand, he began walking with her toward the French doors. "We'll see you later, Mona."

"Sneaky," Elise murmured in admiration. "Definitely sneaky."

"Not at all. I do want to dance with you. And I would infinitely rather do it in a place less crowded."

She stopped, pulling her hand out of his. "Actually," she said when he turned with an inquiring look, "I'd rather not dance, if you don't mind."

He stared at her for a moment, then shook his head. "I know just the thing. Come with me."

He took her hand again, leading her across the terrace and into the carefully tended garden beyond. This was not what Elise had in mind, but she would feel like a fool if she made any more objections.

"You were right," he said as he sat beside her on a smooth marble bench. "This is much better than dancing. We'll be able to get to know each other out here."

She glanced at him from under her lashes, then gave a mental shrug. Pretending they were strangers hadn't occurred to her, but it was one way of getting around the tension that had been between them since their last meeting.

"What do you do when you're not standing around being beautiful?" he asked, smiling down at her.

She gave a soft laugh. "What a smooth line. Did you—"

"Elise!"

"What now?" Garrick groaned in exasperation. "You should carry an answering service around with you. Who in hell is that?"

"That, if I'm not mistaken, is my delightful little sister," Elise said.

In the next second Trish appeared around the corner, her thin face pinched with anger. Trish was the only one of Mona's children who actually resembled her. Trish's hair wasn't quite as red as Mona's and her breasts weren't quite as large, but since Mona had paid dearly for both her hair and her breasts, Trish still had a shot at becoming a carbon copy of her mother.

"Mother is asking for you," Trish said when she reached them. "There are some people she wants you to meet . . . and you should be glad you have a famous name, because if you didn't, she'd make you hide in the closet when her special guests were here."

Elise exhaled a heavy sigh. "I've already been ambushed by Jason and Sharon, and I'm not up to another battle tonight. And if I were, it wouldn't be with you. For heaven's sake, we're not teenagers anymore. You're twenty-two years old. Use a little subtlety in your insults, a little panache."

"What—"

"No, never mind," Elise said, shaking her head. "It's over. You can have her."

"What on earth are you talking about?" asked the redhead, backing away warily.

"It's time to get down and dirty, little sister," said Elise, her voice dry. "This is about Mona. It's always been about Mona. Well, I surrender. She's yours. I hereby bequeath you full rights to our mother."

Apparently Trish hadn't expected Elise to bring it out in the open, and her face showed her confusion. "I don't know what you mean."

"I'll have a contract drawn up in the morning. I no longer recognize Mona as my mother. She's all yours. I will refuse her time, her attention, and anything she's left me in her will. Now, please, will you leave me alone? Will you pretend you don't know me? I've tried for ten years to be a friend to you and Jason and Sharon. I'm tired of trying. I'm tired of going out of my way to spare your feelings when you never give one thought to mine. I'm tired of understanding why you act the way you do, when I get no understanding in return. I give up on you." She waved her hands in the air, weaving a freestyle spell. "Poof, it's done. You're not my baby sister. You're an annoying acquaintance, one whose company I'm no longer obligated to endure."

Trish's expression changed rapidly as she huffed in anger, a junior edition of Mona. Then, swinging around, she stalked off down the path.

Garrick laughed softly. "You're getting feisty, aren't you?"

"You wouldn't know anything about this, since we've only met," she began slowly, "but recently something happened to me, something traumatic, and I decided that from now on I would be myself. I realized that pretense, even for the best of reasons, is not a kindness. Sooner or later people get hurt."

After a moment of silence he reached out and touched her face with his scarred hand. "You've noticed that my hand is disfigured, but it doesn't bother you, does it?"

"No," she said, swallowing the lump in her throat. "It doesn't bother me at all."

Holding her gaze, he slowly leaned forward until their lips brushed.

Elise caught her breath and pulled away from the kiss. "I—The thing is, you see, I'm afraid I don't make love with strangers."

"Were we making love?"

"It sure felt like it to me," she whispered warily. "It felt a lot like it."

"Make an exception, Elise," he said, his voice deep and husky. "Say that for me you'll make an exception. Tonight is a night for change. A night for taking off the gloves. Tonight you're a woman who takes chances. A woman who doesn't do the correct thing. Make an exception, Elise."

"Holy hell," she exclaimed as she found herself more than halfway to the point of agreeing with him.

Standing abruptly, she muttered an unintelligible excuse and rushed away from the stone bench . . . from the dark stranger who was no stranger at all.

In one of the upstairs bathrooms Elise paced for a while, then sat down on a velvet-covered vanity stool to think. She didn't understand why Garrick was doing what he was doing, but even more unsettling was the fact that she didn't understand why she was playing along with him.

At first it had seemed a harmless game, something to help them over the awkwardness of seeing each other again. But out there in the dark, it hadn't felt like a game. It had felt deadly serious. She couldn't let it happen to her again. Another little go-around with Garrick would very likely kill her.

She closed her eyes, and unbidden came the memory of the last two times they had made love. He had as good as told her, down there in the garden, that she could have it all again, all the wildness, all the brilliant flashes of ecstasy.

But at what price? she asked herself. Even if he had finished with Charis, there would be others. And if even the thought of him being with another woman could twist her inside out, what would the reality do to her?

Finding the answer gave her no comfort, and she opened her eyes reluctantly. At that same moment Trish walked into the room.

Elise moaned and stood up, shaking her head as she moved toward the door.

"Elise, wait."

Reluctantly, Elise turned back to face her younger sister. "What do you want?"

Trish moistened her lips, then cleared her throat. "I've been thinking about what you said. About how childish our fighting is. And, well, I'd like to talk to you about everything . . . sometime," she said, her voice dwindling away indecisively.

"Call me when we get back to Dallas," Elise said, her shoulders twitching in a shrug. "Now that we're no longer sisters, maybe we can be friends."

Trish frowned. "You really meant that? That I'm not your sister anymore?"

"I meant it."

"Maybe I need a sister."

Elise pulled the door open. "Let's take it slow. Tomorrow you will probably decide that everything I've said and done tonight is a ploy to get you to drop your guard so I can sneak in and steal Mona's affection."

"I won't," said Trish, her voice stubborn.

"We'll see."

"Elise? I'll call you, okay?"

Elise smiled gently as she walked out the door. "You do that, Trish."

She made her way slowly down the hall. Suddenly she was being jerked to the side. Nearly off her feet, she tumbled against a lean, hard body . . . and then the door slammed shut behind her. A pair of firm, sensual lips started to work their wonders on the side of her neck.

There was no need for her to ask who had pulled her into the closet, who was kissing her.

No one else could start fires burning in her with a single touch. "Garrick, let go of me, you fool. You're not the kind of man who makes love in a linen closet."

"We're strangers, remember?" His husky voice filled the darkness. "You don't know what kind of man I am."

"But I don't make love to strangers . . . remember?"

"I know what you told me, and you know what I told you. Tonight is a night to break the rules. This night will never come again. If we let it get away from us, we could regret it for the rest of our lives. Tomorrow we'll be strangers again. I'll simply be the man you met at a party. But tonight . . . ah, tonight, my beautiful, dear stranger, tonight you can see into my heart and I can see into yours."

She felt herself giving in. Melting.

Pulling herself together, she said, "This is ridiculous. We're in a *closet*, for Pete's sake."

He laughed. "It won't work, Elise. You're weakening. I can feel it. In fact, I can feel everything you're feeling. I can feel the heat building here"—he touched her with one hand, finding the exact spot where the heat was building— "and spreading, rising to here, making these hard." With one move he pushed her strapless gown down to her waist. "Sweet heaven, I love them hard . . . hard against my tongue, against my hands, my chest. I love it when they swell, when I can feel the passion filling them up so that they spill over my fingers."

Without her consent her fingers were tearing at his shirt, trying to free the buttons so she could feel the heat of his flesh against her hands, against her breasts. Sounds of impatience and desire became mixed in her throat, reflecting the urgent need that was growing out of control.

Then someone knocked on the door of the closet.

Garrick, his breath coming in harsh gasps, clasped her neck with one hand. "Please tell me that's just a love sound I've never heard you make before."

A weak laugh caught in her throat as she leaned her forehead against his shoulder. "Sorry," she said, "it wasn't me."

As she tried to pull her dress into some kind of order, Garrick opened the door a fraction of an inch.

"Yes?" he said, as though he were opening his front door to an annoying salesman.

Trish's voice came through the crack. "I'm sorry to interrupt, but Mother has the National Guard out looking for you both. I thought you would rather have me interrupt you than one of the guests."

"Yes . . . thank you, Trish," he said, then closed the door in her face.

She felt him turn around to face her, but he didn't come closer. After a moment he said, "I'm not staying here tonight. I have a room at the Riata. Eight-oh-three. I'll be there all evening, Elise. It doesn't matter how late. I'll be awake."

Then he turned and opened the door, letting

in a flood of light before he closed it behind him.

Elise stood where he had left her, then slowly her knees gave way and she slumped down to the floor, leaning her head back against a shelf.

He could have taken her, right there in Mona's linen closet. She would have let him—

A sound of self-contempt caught in her throat. Let him? *Let* him? Another couple of minutes and she would have thrown *him* to the floor.

But he didn't let it happen. Like the civilized man he was, he was giving her a choice. He was forcing her to make a rational decision. He was asking her to take responsibility for her own actions. And later she wouldn't be able to say she had been carried away by the heat. She had to make a choice, away from him, away from his touch.

For the rest of the evening, as Elise mingled, she told herself she wouldn't go. That way only led to more pain. And she had already had enough of that to last her a couple of lifetimes. Better safe than sorry, she told herself. Who needs the aggravation?

But at five minutes after midnight she was in the lobby of the Riata.

She could still change her mind, she told herself. She could turn around and leave right now, with no one the wiser.

She could still do the smart thing, she told herself as she stepped out of the elevator on the eighth floor.

Two seconds after she knocked on the door of room 803, he jerked it open. When he saw her, he closed his eyes briefly, tightly. Then he gave her a brilliant smile, and he stepped into the hall, closing the door behind him.

"Where are we going?" she asked as he took her arm.

"We need to talk," he explained.

"Can't we talk in your room?"

He met her eyes. "Can we?"

After a moment she shook her head slowly. "Nooo, I don't suppose we can."

They rode the elevator down to the lobby, and from there they reached the pool. It was after midnight. The pool was closed and the area around it deserted. Taking her hand in his, he began to walk with her around the pool, and as they walked, they talked.

He relived for her episodes from his childhood, from the time when his sister was still alive. Most of the memories were happy ones, but a few obviously had been traumatic. He told her about growing up with parents who wouldn't allow their children to sit at the dinner table until they were in college. About having every word he spoke and every move he made monitored by servants—and always he had been aware that it was his sacred duty to uphold the name of Fane.

It was only after his sister's death that he had decided to make his own rules, to find a code of honor that had something more to do with honor than the stiff etiquette he had been taught by his parents.

It must have been around three in the morning when they stopped talking and sat in lounge chairs that they had pushed close together.

Their conversation was quieter, but no less intense. By the light of a waning moon, Elise told Garrick about her dear, gentle father, about the time she had caught Mona in bed with the gardener's son, and about the time she had had to sit home on the night of the junior high school dance because she was taller than every boy in her class.

With lazy laughter in her voice, she told him about playing Tarzan with Max and Annie. Max had been Tarzan, and gentle little Annie had been given the role of Jane, but Elise's role had constantly changed. Although she had refused to be Tarzan's faithful chimpanzee companion, she had been a savage warrior, the leader of a gang of gunrunners, and the evil queen of a lost civilization.

They were still sitting by the pool when the sun came up the next morning. The night was over and they hadn't made love. They had barely touched.

Rising to his feet, he pulled her out of her chair. "You're tired. I'll take you back to Mona's."

At her mother's front door he took her into his arms and kissed her, a kiss so gentle, so giving, it brought tears to her eyes.

"I'm glad you took a chance," he said quietly. "I'm glad you broke the rules for me."

"So am I."

And she was. Whatever happened in the future, whatever ills or fortunes were in store for them, she was glad that she had had this night with him.

Ten

The next morning when Elise opened her eyes, a tidal wave of warmth washed over her, because as soon as she opened her eyes, she remembered the night before, the night she had spent with a gentle, loving stranger, a stranger who was her husband.

Wrapping her arms around her waist, she hugged the memories to her, enclosing the warmth, reveling in the remembered sound of his . . .

She sat up abruptly, shoving the covers aside with trembling fingers. Seconds later she was rushing around the bedroom, throwing clothes into her leather suitcase with panic dogging her every step.

She couldn't remember whether or not Mona had said Garrick would be at the house today, but Elise wasn't going to wait around to find out. She was going to get out while she had the chance. She couldn't see him.

Moments earlier, as she had lain in bed remembering the hours they had spent beside the pool, the truth had struck her, struck her hard.

Last night Garrick had refused to seduce her physically, but he had done something much, much worse. He had seduced her emotionally.

Out in the open, while her guard was down, he had dangled what she wanted most before her eyes. He had shown her the man she loved as she had never dreamed he could be. Open and warm and vibrantly alive.

But the worst of it was that he made her doubt her own values. He had made her wonder if faithfulness in a partner was really necessary. He had made her wonder if infidelity was quite as bad as she had believed it was.

She couldn't let it happen again. Elise was aware of her weaknesses where Garrick was concerned. And so was he.

She knew the strength of his determination. She had witnessed it over and over again in the courtroom. When he believed in something, when he wanted a certain result, he would stop at nothing to achieve it.

The gentle man she had seen last night would be nowhere in sight when it came to that kind of battle. Garrick would pull out all the stops. He would remember every one of her weaknesses, and he would use each of them against her. And in the end, he would win.

If she let him. If she let him get close enough to pull her in again.

She wouldn't let it happen, she told herself, her lips tight with determination as she picked up the phone and rang through to Mona's chauffeur.

If Elise let Garrick win, if she gave herself to him again, she would end up losing what little self-respect she had left.

Elise pulled her Mercedes out of her parking space and headed for the freeway. For the past two weeks she had been working around the clock to catch up with the work that had, one way or another, been neglected recently, and she was tired. She couldn't remember ever being so tired.

Several days earlier Elise had received a call from Max. He had talked nonstop for half an hour, telling her all about his new assignment. Quite naturally, he had asked about Garrick, but Elise had put him off. There was nothing Elise could tell him. How many ways can you say it's over?

Trish had also called. Elise and her younger sister didn't exactly have a relationship yet, but neither was there a war. That was progress.

And last but not least, Garrick had called. He had telephoned her more times than she could count, but Elise had taken none of the calls. She wasn't ready yet. She wasn't strong enough yet.

Would she ever be? she wondered, staring straight ahead at the traffic. Would she ever be able to see him without feeling the desperate need she always felt, that she felt now, just thinking of him?

In the two weeks since she had returned from Springfield, Elise had done a lot of thinking. Belatedly, she was recognizing her own culpability. If she had been a better wife, a better companion to him, Garrick wouldn't have turned to Charis. Elise could see that now. And because she could understand, she should have been able to forgive, but she couldn't forgive and she couldn't forget.

Max always said she was too unyielding. Maybe he was right, but Elise didn't know how to be less than she was.

With all her heart she wished she could lay the past to rest, put it behind her and start all over again with Garrick. But how could she trust him in the future, knowing what he had done in the past?

It wouldn't work. She knew herself too well. If they stayed together, she would be constantly checking up on him, looking through his pockets, calling his office to make sure he was where he was supposed to be. She would make their life together a living hell.

If she could go back to the beginning, she would do it differently. She would be the kind of wife he needed so that his scruples would never be put to the test. That way she could have lived her whole life without ever knowing he had this particular flaw.

But they couldn't go back.

Regret brought fresh tears to her eyes. She didn't want to live the rest of her life without Garrick, and her need made her angry. Was this how Max felt about Annie? Was Elise going to spend the rest of her life wandering, looking for something she would never find?

Half an hour later, as she entered the dark house, she thought, for the first time in a long time, of the one who was waiting to love her. And as though thinking of him had allowed him entrance, his warmth surrounded her like a physical presence.

And then, standing in the dark hallway, Elise did something she had never done before. She rejected the waiting love. She willed the warmth away from her.

Because now she knew that she didn't want this nameless, faceless, loving man. She wanted Garrick. She had always wanted Garrick. And no man, no matter how wonderful and patient, no matter how open and loving, would ever be able to replace him in her heart.

She walked into the living room, and moving to the end table beside the sofa, she switched on the lamp. A split second later she clasped a hand to the heart that leaped wildly in her chest.

Garrick was sitting in one of the chairs in front of the fireplace. He didn't turn his head to look at her, but continued staring into the cold, empty hearth.

"Why haven't you been answering the telephone?" he asked quietly. "When I call here, I get the answering machine, and when I call your office, Pat says you're not taking any calls."

She stared at him, taking note of the deep lines of weariness in his face, the grim tightness about his mouth.

Dropping her briefcase to the floor, she sat down on the sofa. "I didn't think there was anything to talk about."

After a moment of electric silence he said, "We talked an entire night away in Springfield. Neither of us could stop talking. There always seemed to be something more to share with each other." He turned his head to look at her. "But now you say we have nothing to talk about."

Exhaling a slow breath, she rested her head against the back of the sofa. "I've done a lot of thinking in the last two weeks . . . you wouldn't believe how much thinking I've done. I've dreamed up all kinds of excuses for what happened, trying to make it seem not so bad. But none of them would stick, Garrick. In the end, it always came back to—"

"Excuses for what happened?" he repeated, his face genuinely puzzled. "Explain that to me, please. I assume you're talking about a specific thing I've done, a specific sin I've committed, and I think I have a right to know what it is."

Staring at the ceiling, she said, "I'm talking about your relationship with Charis, Garrick. All those nights you spent with her. All those nights I spent alone."

He rose to his feet abruptly. "That was a

mistake. I know that now. A miscalculation on my part. I should never have— But there's something you don't understand. That night we talked by the pool, there was something I left out. I may have left it out intentionally, I don't know. There are things that will always be difficult for me to talk about. Paula is one of them."

She raised her head to stare at him. "Paula? I thought we were talking about Charis."

He shook his head restlessly. "It's all connected. If Paula hadn't been the way she was, I would never have gone to Charis and left you alone. Never."

The reasons didn't matter, she told herself. No reason was good enough to excuse what he did. He had betrayed her. He had made love to another woman. And that was all that mattered.

Only it wasn't, she admitted silently. Right or wrong, she wanted to hear his reasons.

"Tell me about it," she said slowly. "Tell me about Paula . . . and about Charis."

He shoved his left hand in his pocket; then, realizing what he had done, pulled it out again. That would be a hard habit for him to break. He didn't know what to do with the hand he had kept hidden for so long.

After moving to stand with his back to the fireplace, he quietly began speaking. "Paula was delicate, physically and emotionally . . . but I told you all about that. What I didn't tell you was that when she was eighteen, she became engaged to a young man my parents didn't approve of. And they were very vocal, almost abusive, in their disapproval. Paula stood up to them. She told them if they couldn't accept Brad, she would have nothing more to do with them." He drew in a short breath. "I've told you enough about my parents for you to guess what happened. They refused to accept her fiancé, and she moved out. She left with Brad and disappeared completely. I was only fifteen at the time, but I looked for her. I went to the places she told me Brad had taken her, but no one had seen or heard of her. Six months later we found her, or rather the mental hospital she was in found us. She had finally become rational enough to tell someone who she was."

He moved his shoulders gingerly, as though the memories were weighing on him. "My parents moved her to a better hospital, but it was over five years before she could come home again. My parents, my aunts and uncles, the whole family, stopped talking about her. It was as though she ceased to exist. And I wasn't allowed to talk about her either. No one could know that the Fanes had a 'mental case' in the family.

"I visited her when I could, but it wasn't very often, not until I got my own car and could drive myself." He smiled. "I remember the day she learned she was coming home. She was giddy with happiness, dreaming up all kinds of wonderful things that were going to happen as soon as she came home. But of course they were only fantasies. Mother and Father didn't want her anymore. She had disgraced them. That was how she got her little cabin in the woods. Back there, she was out of sight. Back there, they could forget she lived."

He glanced at Elise and ran his fingers abruptly through his hair, as though irritated with himself. "I guess you're wondering what all this has to do with Charis."

"I think I'm beginning to understand," she said, meeting his gaze. "When Walter left, and Charis broke down so completely, it reminded you of Paula, didn't it?"

He nodded. "It was like seeing it happen all over again. With Paula, I was too young and too uninformed to do anything. I couldn't help her." He closed his eyes. "It was as if I would be repaying the debt I owed Paula, if only I could do something to help Charis."

Opening his eyes, he turned to look at her. "Can you understand that? Does it make any kind of sense? I know I left you alone all those nights, but Charis needed me. You didn't."

Something in her expression caused him to frown. "Maybe you could get along without me so easily because I never let you see who I really was. What I mean— Well, you see, if I had known at the beginning how important opening up to you would be, I would have forced myself to do it. But I didn't know. I didn't know until recently how important it was. I thought the only thing between us was sex. . . . I know, I know, and I'm sorry. That was stupid of me. I thought the only reason you married me was because you liked what I did to you, you liked how I made you feel."

"There was that," she admitted wryly.

He gave a short laugh. "Yes, I know. There was that. But there could have been more, if I had only known. Edmund Spenser said a man who strives to touch a star often stumbles on a straw. That's what it felt like, Elise. I had my eyes on a star, and I just kept screwing up."

She shook her head in bewilderment, not understanding half of what he said. She couldn't understand the sudden intensity in his voice, intensity that was causing him to become almost incoherent.

"You went to Charis out of pity," she said slowly. "I can understand. I can see what made you want to take care of her, want to be there for her so she wouldn't fall apart completely. But, Garrick, that doesn't explain why you slept with her. You haven't said one word, *not one damn word*, about why you felt it was necessary to make love to her!"

She stood up, as surprised by the explosive anger she suddenly felt as he obviously would be when he heard her next words. "That's enough," she said, turning to walk away. "You've told me what you came to tell me—"

Grasping her arm, he swung her around. But there was no anger in his face. His midnight eyes were filled with confusion. And something that looked very much like despair.

"What the hell? This doesn't make sense. Elise, I never, *never* made love to her. Do you hear me? I never so much as touched her. Yes, I held her when she cried. I would have done that for anyone . . . and so would you. But anything else—" He broke off to shake his head sharply from side to side. "There was never anything between us. I knew she was promiscuous, but I also know that's one of the symptoms of emotional instability, so I couldn't reject her because of that. Did you think, just because I was spending time with her—"

"No," she said, her voice calmer now. Because she had seen his face, and she knew the truth. "I believed you were having an affair with Charis because Charis told me you were having an affair with her."

"What?"

"Yeah," she said dryly. "Charis lied. What a surprise."

It was all so clear now. Elise had known from the beginning that Charis was in the habit of lying. She had known, yet still she had accepted the woman's word as gospel.

"You believe me?" Garrick asked.

"Oh yes, I believe you."

"Then why do you look like that? Why do you look so sad?" There was desperation in his voice, anxiety in his dark eyes. "Is that not enough? Is there some other reason you wanted out of our marriage?"

Turning away from him, she bit her lip to keep it from trembling. She had to be strong now. If they were to have a new beginning, if they were going to get another chance at a life together, it had to be done correctly this time.

The relief and overwhelming joy she had felt when she knew he hadn't been unfaithful to her had too quickly dissipated in a cloud of doubt. If they had been closer, if Garrick had loved her, and if she had acknowledged her love for him, there would have been no misunderstanding. But as long as the same faults existed in their relationship, other misunderstandings were sure to occur.

She was certain now that Garrick wanted their marriage to work. He had shown her how much when he had opened up to her that night by the pool. But it still wasn't enough. They would have to go back to square one. They would have to begin with a proper courtship. And if she couldn't make him fall in love with her, with the real Elise, certified product of Weiden Street, then they would have to give it up.

The thought broke her heart. She didn't want to give up. But how could she force a man to fall in love with her? Especially a man like Garrick. There was no—

She felt his fingers on her shoulder just moments before she was hauled around to face him. To face a man she had never seen before. His strong features were twisted with some violent emotion, his eyes bright with unshed tears.

"It's time for it to stop, Elise," he said, each word ground out harshly. "It's time for the pain to stop. It's time for me to stop hoping. I can't take any more . . . two solid years of loving you, of waiting for you to turn to me, waiting for you to love me back. It's got to stop now. You can do it. You can make it stop. Whatever you've done to me, undo it. Take it away. It's driving me out of my mind!"

Dropping his hand, he swiveled around and headed for the front door.

Garrick was leaving. He was leaving her again, and all she could do was watch in stunned silence.

It had been Garrick all along. The one who waited so patiently to love her, the one who waited to receive her love, the one who wanted her so desperately. It was Garrick. He had been right there beside her, and she had never once opened her eyes to see him.

"See me, Elise," he had told her. "Open your eyes and see *me*."

"*Garrick!*" she screamed, running toward the open front door.

When she caught up with him, he had already started his car and was pulling out of the driveway. Without hesitating, she dived at the door on the passenger side and wrenched it open.

"Don't go," she said, her voice pleading as tears ran freely down her face. "You can't leave me now."

Without looking at her, he shoved the gearshift into "park" and leaned his head against the steering wheel, closing his eyes. "I'm tired, Elise."

Her throat constricted painfully, her heart going wild in her chest. "Tired of loving me?" she whispered, afraid to hear the answer. "I didn't know, Garrick. I swear to God I didn't know. We said words in the beginning, and I'm sure love came in there somewhere, at least I know it did on my side. But somewhere along the way the words got lost, and I thought the feelings were lost along with them. But we were the ones who were lost, not the feelings, not the love. Never the love.

"I— I don't think I can live without you, Garrick. I was almost ready to beg you to come back, even when I thought you had been sleeping with Charis. Doesn't that tell you something? Doesn't that show you?" she shouted, trying to penetrate the icy cloak he had thrown around himself.

Garrick raised his head from the steering wheel and slowly turned it toward her. The moment their eyes met, his face twisted, and he jerked her across the seat, into his arms.

"Elise, sweet heaven, *Elise*." He groaned, burying his face in her throat. "I thought it was all gone. I thought I had lost you. And—" He broke off and shook his head. "I didn't know what to do, where to go. It's scary, Elise, but I have no life without you."

"I know . . . I know," she murmured as she spread urgent kisses across his strong face. "But it's okay. It didn't happen. We didn't let it happen. We won't ever let it happen."

Covering his mouth with hers, she dipped her

tongue deep inside in an attempt to pull him away from the specter of emptiness they both had faced moments earlier. A moan came from deep in his throat, and he grasped her waist, pulling her into his lap, moving his hips upward to welcome her.

It took only seconds for their passions to build to a frenzy. It had always been that way between them—and now she knew it always would be.

When she felt a button hit her cheek, she glanced down, watching as his scarred fingers pushed first her blouse, then her bra, out of the way to find the naked, warm flesh.

"The backseat?" he said, his voice a hoarse whisper.

Moments later, as they lay together in the backseat of his Mercedes, he stopped for a moment to fold the blouse he had just ripped off her and lay it across the back of the seat.

Because above all Garrick was a civilized man.

THE EDITOR'S CORNER

What a joy it is to see, hear, smell and touch spring once again! Like a magician, nature is pulling splendors out of an invisible hat—and making us even more aware of romance. To warm you with all the radiance and hopefulness of the season, we've gathered together a bouquet of six fabulous LOVESWEPTs.

First, from the magical pen of Mary Kay McComas, we have **KISS ME, KELLY,** LOVESWEPT #462. Kelly has a rule about dating cops—she doesn't! But Baker is a man who breaks the rules. In the instant he commands her to kiss him he seizes control of her heart—and dares her to tell him she doesn't want him as much as he wants her. But once Kelly has surrendered to the ecstasy he offers, can he betray that passion by seducing her to help him with a desperate, dirty job? A story that glows with all the excitement and uncertainties of true love.

With all things green and beautiful about to pop into view, we bring you talented Gail Douglas's **THE BEST LAID PLANS,** LOVESWEPT #463. Jennifer Allan has greenery *and* beauty on her mind as she prepares to find out exactly what Clay Parrish, an urban planner, intends to do to her picturesque hometown. Clay is a sweet-talker with an irrepressible grin, and in a single sizzling moment he breaches Jennifer's defenses. Once he begins to understand her fears, he wages a glorious campaign to win her trust. A lot of wooing . . . and a lot of magic—in a romance you can't let yourself miss.

In Texas spring comes early, and it comes on strong—and so do the hero and heroine of Jan Hudson's **BIG AND BRIGHT,** LOVESWEPT #464. Holt Berringer is one of the good guys, a long lean Texas Ranger with sin-black eyes and a big white Stetson. When the entrancing spitfire Cory Bright has a run-in with some bad guys, Holt admires her refusal to hide from threats on her life and is determined to cherish and protect her. Cory fears he will be too much like the domineering macho men she's grown to dislike, but Holt is as tender as he is tough. Once Cory proves that she can make it on her own, will she be brave enough to settle for the man she really wants? A double-barrelled delight from the land of yellow roses.

Peggy Webb's **THAT JONES GIRL**, LOVESWEPT #465, is a marvelous tale about the renewal of an old love between a wild Irish rover and a beautiful singer. Brawny wanderer Mick Flannigan had been Tess Jones's first lover, best friend, and husband—until the day years before when he suddenly left her. Now destiny has thrown them together again, but Tess is still too hot for Mick to handle. She draws him like a magnet, and he yearns to recapture the past, to beg Tess's forgiveness . . . but can this passion that has never died turn into trust? For Peggy's many fans, here is a story that is as fresh, energetic, and captivating as a spring morning.

Erica Spindler's enchanting **WISHING MOON**, LOVESWEPT #466, features a hero who gives a first impression that belies the real man. Lance Alexander seems to be all business, whether he is hiring a fund-raiser for his favorite charity or looking for a wife. When he runs into the cocky and confident Madi Muldoon, she appears to be the last person he would choose to help in the fight to save the sea turtles—until she proves otherwise and he falls under the spell of her tawny-eyed beauty. Still Lance finds it hard to trust in any woman's love, while Madi thinks she has lost her faith in marriage. Can they both learn that wishes made on a full moon—especially wishes born of an irresistible love for each other—always come true? A story as tender and warm as spring itself.

In April the world begins to move outdoors again and it's time to have a little fun. That's what brings two lovers together in Marcia Evanick's delightful **GUARDIAN SPIRIT**, LOVESWEPT #467. As a teenager Josh Langly had been the town bad boy; now he is the local sheriff. When friends pair him with the bewitching dark-haired Laura Ann Bryant for the annual scavenger hunt, the two of them soon have more on their minds than the game.

Forced by the rules to stay side by side with Josh for a weekend, Laura is soon filled with a wanton desire for this good-guy hunk with the devilish grin. And though Josh is trying to bury his bad boy past beneath a noble facade, Laura enchants him beyond all reason and kindles an old flame. Another delectable treat from Marcia Evanick.

And (as if this weren't enough!) be sure not to miss three unforgettable novels coming your way in April from Bantam's spectacular new imprint, FANFARE, featuring the best in women's popular fiction. First, for the many fans of Deborah Smith, we have her deeply moving and truly memorable historical **BELOVED WOMAN**. This is the glorious story of a remarkable Cherokee woman, Katherine Blue Song, and an equally remarkable frontiersman Justis Gallatin. Then, making her debut with FANFARE, Jessica Bryan brings you a spellbinding historical fantasy, **ACROSS A WINE-DARK SEA**. This story has already wowed *Rendezvous* magazine, which called Jessica Bryan "a super storyteller" and raved about the book, describing it as "different, exciting, excellent . . ." The critically-acclaimed Virginia Brown takes readers back to the wildest days of the Wild West for a fabulous and heartwarming love story in **RIVER'S DREAM**.

All in all, a terrific month of reading in store for you from FANFARE and LOVESWEPT!

Sincerely,

Carolyn Nichols

Carolyn Nichols,
Publisher,
LOVESWEPT
Bantam Books
666 Fifth Avenue
New York, NY 10103

THE LATEST IN BOOKS AND AUDIO CASSETTES

Paperbacks

☐	28671	**NOBODY'S FAULT** Nancy Holmes	$5.95
☐	28412	**A SEASON OF SWANS** Celeste De Blasis	$5.95
☐	28354	**SEDUCTION** Amanda Quick	$4.50
☐	28594	**SURRENDER** Amanda Quick	$4.50
☐	28435	**WORLD OF DIFFERENCE** Leonia Blair	$5.95
☐	28416,	**RIGHTFULLY MINE** Doris Mortman	$5.95
☐	27032	**FIRST BORN** Doris Mortman	$4.95
☐	27283	**BRAZEN VIRTUE** Nora Roberts	$4.50
☐	27891	**PEOPLE LIKE US** Dominick Dunne	$4.95
☐	27260	**WILD SWAN** Celeste De Blasis	$5.95
☐	25692	**SWAN'S CHANCE** Celeste De Blasis	$5.95
☐	27790	**A WOMAN OF SUBSTANCE** Barbara Taylor Bradford	$5.95

Audio

☐ **SEPTEMBER** by Rosamunde Pilcher
Performance by Lynn Redgrave
180 Mins. Double Cassette   45241-X $15.95

☐ **THE SHELL SEEKERS** by Rosamunde Pilcher
Performance by Lynn Redgrave
180 Mins. Double Cassette   48183-9 $14.95

☐ **COLD SASSY TREE** by Olive Ann Burns
Performance by Richard Thomas
180 Mins. Double Cassette   45166-9 $14.95

☐ **NOBODY'S FAULT** by Nancy Holmes
Performance by Geraldine James
180 Mins. Double Cassette   45250-9 $14.95

---

60 Minutes to a Better, More Beautiful You!

Now it's easier than ever to awaken your sensuality, stay slim forever—even make yourself irresistible. With Bantam's bestselling subliminal audio tapes, you're only 60 minutes away from a better, more beautiful you!

__ 45004-2   **Slim Forever** $8.95

__ 45035-2   **Stop Smoking Forever** $8.95

__ 45022-0   **Positively Change Your Life** ...$8.95

__ 45041-7   **Stress Free Forever** $8.95

__ 45106-5   **Get a Good Night's Sleep** $7.95

__ 45094-8   **Improve Your Concentration** .$7.95

__ 45172-3   **Develop A Perfect Memory** $8.95

Bantam Books, Dept. LT, 414 East Golf Road, Des Plaines, IL 60016

Please send me the items I have checked above. I am enclosing $_____ (please add $2.50 to cover postage and handling). Send check or money order, no cash or C.O.D.s please. (Tape offer good in USA only.)

Mr/Ms _____

Address _____

City/State_____ Zip _____

LT-2/91

Please allow four to six weeks for delivery.
Prices and availability subject to change without notice.

NEW!
Handsome Book Covers Specially Designed To Fit Loveswept Books

Our new French Calf Vinyl book covers come in a set of three great colors— royal blue, scarlet red and kachina green.

Each 7" × 9½" book cover has two deep vertical pockets, a handy sewn-in bookmark, and is soil and scratch resistant.

To order your set, use the form below.